Knotty by Nature

by

Sherry Youngquist

Cover Art by *Teddi Black*

The Wild Rose Press, Inc.
PO Box 708
Adams Basin, NY 14410-0708
Visit us at www.thewildrosepress.com

Publishing History
First Edition, 2025
Trade Paperback ISBN 978-1-5092-6300-4
Digital ISBN 978-1-5092-6301-1

Published in the United States of America

Dedication

To Erik and Wes

Chapter 1

Moving away from a small town is easy. The hard part is coming back, especially if your grandmother is in prison for embezzling from a beach chair rental business.

Fortunately, my coping skills included coming up with different recipes at my family's bakery and posting the ooey-gooey content on TikTok.

"Happy Wednesday," I called out to my online followers as I spilled brown sugar pretzel bites onto my great-grandmother's butcher block. I brought out another tray, delivering the intoxicating aroma of caramel and roasted popcorn.

Customers lingered at the chalkboard menu. Today's special: pecan pie pretzels with caramel dipping sauce. A woman in a faded T-shirt and joggers stood halfway in the door, hanging her helmet on the handlebars of a weathered beach cruiser. Outside, shopkeepers were sweeping sand from porches, and seagulls called out, the sounds of a small coastal town coming to life in early spring.

Two months ago, returning to my hometown of Seabrook, Georgia, to run my family's bakery was the furthest thing from my mind. I had wanted to be a writer and was living in Atlanta, but my mother had drowned in a kayaking accident before my thirtieth birthday, leaving what had once been a storied eatery along the boardwalk in jeopardy.

Oh, and that part about Gram. She did steal money from the beach chair rental business. Don't ask me how a check to save the turtle hospital appeared for the same amount. On the same day. Townspeople thought it had something to do with my family's legend. Gram's ancestors founded this small coastal town. Add in stories about alchemy, mermaids, and pirates, and you have people believing my ancestors were responsible for the town's tree squirrels having white coats. They even said Gram was a modern-day Robin Hood, blurring the lines between right and wrong.

To our family, though, these remained only stories.

Not that I would have turned down some magic in my life.

I was living in the hometown I swore I would never move back to and sleeping next to my overweight beagle, Mouse, in the cramped apartment above the bakery.

Worst of all, though my mother's body was not found, police were quick to declare her dead, eerily similar to how townspeople gave up when my childhood best friend Brie Kidwell went missing my sophomore year in college.

As I thought about this, I popped a cinnamon-sugar pretzel bite into my mouth and immediately regretted it. I was slightly out of shape after spending most of the last three years sitting at a desk in Atlanta, writing my novel and working at night as an English professor.

I had been willing to live frugally to write and had been in a long-term relationship with yoga pants. The rest of my wardrobe consisted mostly of sleeveless blouses, the shorts I slept in, and a T-shirt from Yosemite that I never returned to an old boyfriend.

Thinking of that last part made me reach for another

pretzel bite.

Two women dressed in business suits walked in carrying reusable grocery bags. They took their time selecting mismatched cafe chairs along a row of tables. I walked out to greet them. "Welcome to the White Squirrel Pretzel."

Donna Jean Brownmiller sauntered in after them. She reached into the "free samples" tray and began chewing on a pretzel bite. She was the owner of the Queen Bean, and she considered me to be one of her loyal subjects. This had been going on since high school.

She studied me coolly. "Casey June Hart. It's been a hot minute since I've seen you."

"Donna," I forced a smile. "What can I get you?"

She wrinkled her nose as she looked around, then grabbed another pretzel bite. "I see you're selling coffee now, too. You know that I've got the best coffee in town."

I pushed a new tray of chocolate hazelnut pretzels in front of her. "This town is big enough for several people to sell coffee. Can I get you a box of pretzel bites to go? I have a new dip, jalapeno pimento cheese."

"No, I'm just meeting someone here." She pursed her lips and walked over to where the women in suits were sitting.

I followed her to their table. "Ladies, can I start you off with drinks and maybe some bratzels? That's a bratwurst wrapped inside a pretzel! They are delicious dipped in raspberry honey mustard."

The women seated with Donna Jean moved some papers to the side of the table. One had red curly hair and Harry Potter glasses. She cradled a purple phone and smiled. I recognized her as Moriah Moore, an attorney in

Seabrook and an adjunct professor at the college who came to our writing club meetings. She also had a booth at the farmer's market where she sold pre-made meals called Beet Boxes that had attracted a lot of attention from health nuts in town. I thought it odd that Donna Jean would hire, or much less be friends with, an attorney who represented her husband when they divorced. Moriah had also been the prosecutor to send my grandmother to prison, but Gram, who so clearly took the money, had it coming.

Moriah moved her glasses to the tip of her nose and looked up at me. "Those sound wonderful. I'll have two."

The other woman had coffee-tea-colored pixie hair. Her jawline tensed. "I'll have the same. Let's also get two pretzel bite variety boxes to go with strawberry cream cheese dipping sauce. I brought some bags to carry them back to the office."

Donna Jean did not make eye contact. As usual, I felt no love lost, spinning on my clogs back to the kitchen to make their food.

From the kitchen, I heard Donna Jean arguing with the red-haired woman. "You'll see," she said. "I run this town. You'll never get business here again." She stomped away and attempted to slam the door on her way out.

Both women looked shaken as they packed their belongings and shifted to get up. I quickly put the bratzels in takeout containers, stacking them on top of the pretzel bite variety boxes. I rushed to their table, and with exchanged sympathetic looks, I helped pack the food into the reusable grocery bags. "I could tell that you probably needed this to go. I included a pint of my new jalapeno pimento cheese dip. Enjoy."

The woman with pixie hair looked down, fetched an envelope, and handed it to me reluctantly. "Casey June Hart. You've been served." She released the envelope into my hands and left two twenty-dollar bills on the table.

"What?" I asked as they hurried out of the bakery.

I tore open the envelope. Donna Jean Brownmiller was suing me.

She was asking a judge to forbid me and my grandmother from using the road my family had used for more than a century to get to our home—a now dilapidated lightkeeper's house at the edge of town. The suit implied that our family never had a legal easement allowing travel through the road that runs along the Brownmiller estate. Donna Jean's mother had passed away earlier this year, leaving Donna Jean as her sole heir.

I sank into one of the cafe chairs and crumpled the paper. A sick feeling came over me as I realized I was going to have to hire an attorney and spend money I didn't have.

I reached for my phone and sent the same text I sent almost every day

—*Wish you were here to help me.*—

I knew there would be no response.

My childhood best friend, Brie Kidwell, went missing during our sophomore year in college. She vanished after a night of celebrating at 13th Street Cafe, a small bar near Savannah College. Final exams were over. There was talk of summer jobs and bonfires on the beach. It had been a balmy evening with a clear sky and a full moon. A group of us had just finished a bucket of cheap beers. I got a ride home with two other girls. Brie had recently broken up with her boyfriend and wanted to enjoy the night air and clear her head. She decided to walk the short distance from the bar to our dorm.

She never made it. In the first days and nights after her disappearance, I texted her almost hourly. I kept texting as we held candlelight vigils, posted flyers, and went door-to-door. Later, my messages were less desperate and more archival. I told her about graduation and what she missed. I sent her messages on holidays and birthdays. More than nine years later, I still texted her, hoping she was still "out there" somewhere. It was also comforting to turn to her about things that I could share with no one else. It was a way to keep her alive.

I stared down at the message that I had sent. Nothing.

I sighed as I breathed in a simple prayer, then typed:
—*Come home, B.*—

An hour later, feeling sorry for myself, I closed the bakery early and sat at a table in the back, eating Lean Cuisine as Mouse lapped up a bowl of dog food mixed with water. I picked up the small microwavable plastic bowl and walked in my wool socks to the front of the bakery and out onto the deck, where there were more cafe tables and chairs. Mouse plodded along after me. I sat next to the front door near a concrete leprechaun guarding the wooden bin used for bulk flour deliveries. The sun was going down, a spring afternoon in pink. I sat for what seemed like twenty minutes, scraping the last of my frozen meal with a fork, listening to the roar of the ocean, thinking of my mom.

An orange tabby cat walked delicately up the path leading from the beach. It purred and leaned on my legs.

against my leg and took off.

We were far away from the touristy parts of Seabrook now. This is what they called the real Georgia coast—mossy oaks and dense brush, the sound of crickets and katydids. Up ahead, I saw it. There was a newly constructed security gate now keeping me from my family's home. I bit my lip, and my heart sank. A sign chained to the gate stated, "No Trespassing. Violators will be prosecuted."

I was still a few yards from the gate and was moving a little slower when the orange cat came back into view and mewed in front of the gate before climbing through and disappearing next to an old shed. Something was lying next to the bottom of the gate, and I squinted to see the same black, round eyeglasses from earlier today lying on the ground. The Harry Potter glasses!

I stepped closer. Moriah Moore was face down in a pint of my jalapeno pimento dip. I called out to her, but there was no response, and my stomach roiled. I turned her over and reached to check her pulse. Nothing. Moriah was cold to the touch. I fumbled to dial 911.

All the air rushed from my lungs, and I couldn't seem to breathe in or out.

With watery eyes, I squatted, then fell to my knees next to her.

Something covered her lips and poked out of her mouth. It was red. It was also bumpy and gnarled. Then, it dawned on me. I lurched to my feet. It was a Carolina Reaper, one of the hottest peppers in the world!

Chapter 2

Blue police lights flashed in the darkness as Seabrook police and first responders secured the scene around the gate. A few townspeople huddled behind yellow crime scene tape and whispered among themselves, straining to see what was going on. Some of those included Moriah Moore's co-workers at her law firm and at the college.

I was wrapped in a blanket and sitting on a deputy's truck tailgate when I heard a familiar voice. Detective Fin Westmoreland was carrying two cups from my favorite food truck, Forgotten Coast Coffee. I sighed, glad to see him, then bit my lip. Our parents had lived across the bay from each other all our lives—my mother raising me in the lightkeeper's house after my father died and his parents bringing up Fin and his brother in a renovated lifesaving station not more than half a mile across the water. We never dated, but he was fiercely protective, costing me more than one chance in high school to go on a date.

"Casey June Hart," he said, handing me one of the cups. "Look who snuck back into town without calling me. How are you?"

"I'm rattled, but I'm okay," I said, surprised at how ragged my voice sounded. Mouse was sound asleep next to me.

Fin had also lived in Atlanta for a while in his early

twenties, after graduating from the FBI Academy. Four years ago, he had taken a bullet in a bank robbery gone bad and moved back to Seabrook with full disability benefits. Early retirement, though, did not suit him, so he was now our town's newest detective and most eligible bachelor. Only a slight limp remained from his injury. He was still as tall, dark, and overconfident as his yearbook photo, maybe more so now that he had turned his father's old gas station into a gym called Cross Grit.

Fin offered me a tired smile. "What happened?"

"I don't know, really. I was walking to the house."

"You know, we found your pimento cheese on Ms. Moore's face. How did a Carolina Reaper get into that dip?" he asked, now in detective mode and making me nervous.

"That's my dip, but I only add jalapenos to my pimento," I said, now quivering and feeling guilty.

"Moriah sent your grandmother to prison. I also know about the lawsuit," said Fin, sipping his coffee. The way he was looking at me made me even more' uncomfortable. Was he implying that I poisoned Moriah? I hardly knew her other than the few times she had attended writing club meetings on campus.

Mouse nuzzled in closer to my leg. Instead of drinking my coffee, I was now mostly using it to warm my hands. If I had ever been a small-town girl who had gotten away and "made it," as they say, I didn't feel like it now. Nearly all of my confidence had left me.

Donna Jean crossed over the yellow crime scene tape and moved between Fin and me. She carried a to-go tray of coffees from Queen Bean, sitting it on the tailgate where I crumpled a little further inward. She took Fin's now mostly empty coffee cup and handed him one from her tray.

"I came as soon as I heard," she said.

Fin raised his eyebrows as he accepted the fresh cup of coffee. He had dated Donna Jean in high school and still regretted it. "Thank you."

She gloated as she crossed her arms, then turned to me. "I heard they found a White Squirrel container. The Seabrook Voice says it killed her."

He took a deep breath and clenched his jaw. "Donna, you know I don't discuss ongoing investigations. Whatever the Voice is putting online, it isn't based on facts."

With that, she grabbed the to-go tray and left to distribute coffee to police and first responders and also hand out her business cards. Donna Jean had a way of turning the grim discovery of a dead body into a town social. Not a lot had changed since high school, including her frosted hair and blue eye shadow. She was still wearing polo shirts and tight jeans. I had the same dark brown hair, shoulder-length, parted to one side and tucked behind one ear. In school, I was always bending my head forward to look out at the teachers from behind tortoiseshell glasses. Now, I looked out at my customers and students from behind the same frames, just through stronger lenses. The cat-eye shape and ginger-red color contrasted with my steel blue eyes.

Fin turned back to me, relieved that Donna Jean had left. "Sorry about that."

I sighed and gently stroked one of Mouse's velvet ears. He was now wrapped like a burrito in the police blanket. He had tucked his nose deep inside. Mouse seemed to sense how upset I was and let out a deep breath of his own and a small whimper.

I looked up to see Sam Shore. He touched my forearm and moved toward Fin.

Sam had on his campus police uniform, which consisted of khaki pants, a button-down shirt, and a college jacket. He wore a badge on his belt but no gun. He looked more serious than when I had seen him earlier, though his hazel-green eyes seemed sympathetic as he crossed one cowboy boot over the other.

Sam extended his hand to Fin. "I head up campus security. Moriah taught for us at night, and I want to help in any way that I can."

Fin looked bothered by Sam's arrival at his crime scene but managed to say, "Much appreciated" before turning to speak with a crime scene technician who was labeling the plastic bag containing my dip.

I felt a warm hand on my shoulder and turned to see one of my closest friends, Nissy Tombly, holding a small pastry box from her cafe, Lemon Meringue. She side-hugged me. "Thought you could use the company. I was closing up when I heard."

Nissy handed me a sandwich and a butterscotch bar and squeezed in between Mouse and me on the tailgate. She was her usual Nissy with her unruly strawberry blonde hair and freckles. She was what you called wash and wear. She liked the basics: T-shirts, blue jeans, and flip-flops.

"Thanks," I finally croaked. "I need all the friends I can get tonight. I am really doubting whether moving back to Seabrook was a good idea."

Then, a waterfall of tears started, and I cried on her shoulder.

She had one arm around me and another around Mouse. "You don't know how strong you are until that's all you have. Just be yourself. You'll get through this."

My phone dinged, and I flipped it over. I swiped to see a message from an unknown number. Someone had sent a photo of Mouse taken this evening as he slept next to me on the tailgate. They had drawn an X on each of Mouse's eyes.

Underneath, there was a text:

—*Keep out. Knot kidding.*—

I shuddered and pulled Mouse in closer, leaving a protective hand on him. I showed Nissy, and we looked at each other.

Fin, who seemed to notice, walked back over.

After showing him, he asked to take a picture of the text. "It's a threat, Casey June, and we're going to take it seriously. We may find out who sent this or whether you already had it on your phone."

Fin was back in detective mode and was still treating me like a suspect. He added, "I need you to come down to the station tomorrow to answer more questions. I'll drive you home tonight."

I hadn't noticed, but Sam was back in our circle around the tailgate. "I'll drive Casey June," he said. "No problem at all. In fact, we're neighbors. I just moved into the house next to the bakery."

Fin looked down and shook his head. "You're new to Seabrook, and we don't know you at all. We take care of our own here. I will drive her."

At this, Nissy piped up and said she had already decided she would take me home, which seemed to satisfy both men. She offered to let me spend the night at her house, but I knew I couldn't accept.

As we were walking to Nissy's car, someone was walking toward us in the dark. I was holding Mouse in my arms, and he stirred.

Mouse stuck his head up and sniffed the air, then let out a pitiful bark.

The shadowy figure in front of us wore a white gold necklace that sparkled with each step closer to the police lights.

"Gram?" I said.

My grandmother, Icy Faye Echols, stood before us, dressed in a purple velvet duster that nearly fell to the ground. Underneath, she wore a long, flowy black blouse and trousers. She always wore black ballet slippers. Her beautiful white hair, as usual, fell all around her brown face in long ringlets. She looked like a silvery Gullah goddess with large gold hoops dangling from her one cleft earlobe and a single diamond from the other. Her African ancestors, former slaves, were as much a part of the sea islands as the longleaf pine, red cedar, and cabbage palm. And she seemed to wear those exotic colors on every inch of her body.

I was stunned. "I thought you didn't get out until next spring?"

"Early release," she said, turning around with her hands in the air. "Good behavior or something like that," she added, with a twinkle in her eye.

Here I was, face-to-face with the woman who had helped raise me. She had a way with almost everything. Plants, animals. She taught me about the ocean, planets, moons, and stars. Even the dead, helping me keep memories of my father, Joaquin, alive when I was a child. Her "ways," though, often landed her in trouble. She was always pulling for the underdog and would "redistribute resources" (her words, not mine) to help those who really needed it.

Icy Faye pulled me in for a generous hug, and I squeezed her hard.

I was relieved to have her home, but the thought of Nissy's offer to stay the night was more tempting now than ever.

All I wanted to do was crawl into bed and hide underneath the covers.

Chapter 3

The next morning, after a fitful sleep, I woke at four o'clock and dragged my feet into the apartment kitchen. I found Mouse chewing on an old flip-flop, or what was left of one. He lifted his head and rose from the mess on the floor. After a down-dog stretch and grunt, he waddled to the door and made pitiful whining noises.

"You need out?" I asked, patting his head and reaching for his leash.

We walked down from the apartment on the cast iron spiral staircase and into the bakery before heading out onto the front deck. From there, we took the path to the beach and down to the dark water. I was still thinking about the threatening text from last night, letting out a sigh as sandpipers and seagulls darted in and out of the water. The sound of the ocean and the ebb and flow on my bare feet were rhythmic and had a calming effect on me. I closed my eyes and breathed in deeply.

A few minutes later, I walked back to the bakery and led Mouse up into the tiny apartment above. I started the kettle and looked at the kitchen counter, which was cluttered with empty boxes from two of my favorite non-pretzel foods, Lean Cuisine and cereal. I found a clean mug and my favorite Chai black tea. When the kettle whistled, I poured the water over the tea and breathed in the scent of cinnamon and cardamom. Gram was fast asleep on the couch.

I relived the previous night's events and sighed. As much as I wanted to, I didn't have time to wallow in self-pity or go back to bed. I thought for a moment of closing the bakery for the day, posting something online about illness, but most of the town already knew about Moriah, and as I scrolled through my phone, I saw the Seabrook Voice had posted a picture of the pint of pimento cheese at the crime scene. My name wasn't in the newsfeed, but the White Squirrel Pretzel sticker was featured prominently on the pint. *Thanks for helping promote local business*, I thought sarcastically.

To make matters worse, today was Thursday, which meant selling pretzels at the farmer's market. I needed time to prepare.

After a quick shower and change into my daily uniform I had brought with me from Atlanta—black yoga pants, sleeveless blouse, cardigan, clogs—I headed downstairs to the bakery, leaving Gram to snore on the couch and Mouse in his bed below her.

I took each stair slowly, careful not to wake either of them.

As I descended into the bakery, the windows were just getting that first light of the day. I walked through and preheated two of the ovens to 350 Fahrenheit, then covered four baking sheets with parchment paper. I heated a can of beer on the stovetop and added brown sugar and yeast.

Into the commercial mixer went sugar, butter, salt, and the beer mixture. I added the last contents of a bag of bulk bread flour. I was going to need more flour. I knew that our weekly delivery of three fifty-pound flour bags would be waiting for me this morning in the bin by the front door—the regular King Arthur bread flour and one each of Sir Lancelot Hi-Gluten and Sir Galahad Artisan—so I walked out to check. This morning, though, only the two specialty flours had been left. King Arthur was missing. That had happened before, so I ferried the remaining knights in one at a time and finished adding flour to the mixer.

The dough was sticky. I added a little more flour until it became elastic. I took out small amounts of dough and rolled out thin ropes. Some pieces would be for Irish knots, others for pretzels. Some of the dough would be left over for pretzel bites and for wrapping brats and hotdogs.

I left the dough to rise and walked out to the deck to see the sun just coming up over the horizon. I leaned against one of the tables.

Hazel, the white squirrel that lived in my tree, trotted into view along the privacy fence. She looked at me inquisitively, turning her head as she came up on two legs.

"The day hasn't even started yet, and I'm down by three," I told her. I was worried about Gram, worried about the bakery's reputation, and worried I could go to jail next. Who would want to use our pimento cheese dip to kill someone? What was Moriah doing out there at night by the gate?

I reached for a soft pretzel in my cardigan pocket and broke off a small piece for Hazel. She made one small move toward it on the table, watching me.

I sat in relaxed silence with Hazel, then walked back inside, turning to see her sprint to the pretzel piece and take her reward.

Back in the bakery, I put the coffee on, then uploaded a picture of the pretzels while they were baking, letting my social media followers know today's special: garlic parm pretzels. "Are you a pretzel or bite kinda person? Either way, we've got you covered! We're at the farmer's market until 11:00. Stop by the bakery until 3:00."

I was taking the baking sheets out of the oven when I heard the front door and looked over the kitchen counter to see Nissy walking in with a covered dish.

"I thought you could use a pick-me-up after last night," she said, steadying her dish onto one of the cafe tables.

I filled two mugs with coffee. "You have no idea."

Nissy uncovered the dish, revealing one of the biggest reasons her pies were known as far away as Atlanta—maple bacon breakfast pie.

I brought out plates and forks, and we dug in. She had been with me through everything. The death of my father. My mother's eccentric ways. My grandmother often landing in trouble to help her causes. Ridicule in high school for my mostly vintage wardrobe.

Nissy never thought for a moment that my family was weird. She also never questioned the fact that I had hired my ex, Calvin Cunningham, to work a few mornings each week in the bakery. Cal had been the guy who was sensitive and vulnerable enough to imagine having children with, but whose only source of income had been baking bread with brewer's yeast at the Gasper River Brewery. I had loved his beard and organic coffee. I had not enjoyed stumbling over his craft beer-making kit next to the breakfast table, nor his pauses to fix his handlebar mustache. Also, he was a little bit of a bad boy ex. He cheated on me during our last semester in college.

Soon, Cal walked in as we boxed the leftover pie and

gathered our dishes to take to the kitchen. He usually came on Saturday and Sunday mornings to help with the brunch crowd. Those were his days off at the Sea Turtle Hospital, where he worked part-time as a veterinary assistant.

Cal had long since shaved his beard and handlebar mustache. He had a mop of thick brown wavy hair and dark blue eyes. He wore a threadbare public radio T-shirt, hiking shorts, and river sandals. He pushed horn-rimmed frames on his nose and rubbed what looked to be a three-day beard. Though his clothes screamed hipster college dropout with a devil-may-care attitude, Cal had graduated from veterinary school and was serious about his research on sea turtles.

"Morning," he said, pushing past us and heading directly for the magnetic poetry wall. I had recently added it to one side of the dining area.

It was his daily habit—writing a haiku. He arranged the words: Ocean in May, roaring to life angrily, then sleeping all day.

Nissy and I watched Cal.

Finally, I had to ask him. "To what do we owe the pleasure on a Thursday morning? Are you here because you heard about Gram?"

"Maybe," said Cal. He gave a cat-ate-a-canary smile. "Or maybe I heard about what happened last night."

I rubbed my head. Then Nissy and I exchanged amused looks. She turned to leave a short time later and reminded me to stop in at her pie shop. "We added pie-flavored smoothies to the menu, and they are a hit."

I kissed her cheek, and she headed out the door to the opposite end of the street to open Lemon Meringue and start her day.

I reached for my phone. Not wanting to leave Brie out of the fun, I texted:

—*Cal flirts, but it's impossible. He refuses to grow up.*—

I stared down at the screen, always waiting a few seconds after sending. I swiped to look at a picture of Brie and me in high school, the year we both had braces.

I took a picture of Cal's poem and sent it to her. —*I know. It's good to have him back. With all that has been going on, I feel safer with him here. Still, he's Cal.* —

By 6:30, there was only one person sitting at the bar, which was worrying, considering how the townspeople had lumped our bakery in with Moriah's murder.

A tourist came in at about 7:00 for a pretzel breakfast sandwich and coffee. She snapped a selfie in front of the chalkboard menu that included our slogan: "Authentically Local. Seriously Wicked." I forced a smile, surveying our empty dining room. What was supposed to be a coastal farmhouse feel of whitewashed wood and black cast iron looked more like a jail cell today. *Our new slogan: Tragically Caught up in Local Murder. Seriously Going Out of Business.*

By 7:15, the dining area was empty, and my head began to throb. That's when my grandmother descended the stairs in a hot pink shawl; her usual black clothes were underneath. She wore a dazzling mix of orange beads around her neck.

Mouse trotted along after her, part of her processional. She was, after all, the grand dame of the bakery.

Cal was the first to notice. "Good morning, sunshine."

Gram took his hands in hers and squeezed them, then led him to one of the cafe tables to catch up. Those two, I thought. They pick right back up where they left off.

I brought a carafe of coffee for them to share and filled a mug for each of them. I turned to Gram. "What do you want on your first day back?" I asked brightly.

"Toasted coconut with chocolate hazelnut. Warmed!"

"Of course."

I turned back into the kitchen and began prepping two soft pretzels. First, they went into the oven to warm. Then, I brushed them with butter and sprinkled toasted coconut on top. I plated them with a cup of chocolate hazelnut spread and a side of sliced strawberries. Though not requested, I made a pitcher of mimosas, knowing how much they had to catch up on. Cal was good for Gram. The more I thought about it, Cal, who could sometimes be hesitant to follow his dreams, could use a little of her influence, though that last thought scared me a little.

I brought the food out to their table, and they hushed as I approached, sharing some secret of one kind or another. I was used to this. Kindred spirits. I turned to let them have their fun.

Besides, I had been putting off calling an attorney about the lawsuit, something that I still didn't have the heart to tell Gram about. With no one else in the bakery except her and Cal, I walked to the kitchen and pulled out a piece of paper with a phone number for one of Seabrook's best attorneys, Kit Westmoreland. He was Fin's younger brother by two years and had been my junior prom date.

I punched in his number and sucked in a deep breath.

A soft voice on the other end of the line answered. "Kit Westmoreland's office."

"This is Casey June Hart. Is Kit in this morning?"

"No, but you can leave a message."

I filled in his secretary on everything. The lawsuit, the No Trespassing sign, even the fact that there was now a murder investigation. She took my number and told me to stop by the office with a copy of the lawsuit.

After the call, Mouse appeared at my side and was reminding me it was time to head to the farmer's market. Cal had just left so he could set up his own booth at the market. He sold various blends of dried herbs and spices.

I took off my apron, and Gram reached for it before I could hang it on a hook next to the broom closet. She smiled as she tied it around her waist. "I can take it from here."

I kissed her on the cheek and started loading bakery boxes, then took them to the garage.

When I had moved back to Seabrook, I had brought the bicycle I used in Atlanta. It was my go-to transportation around town. For the farmer's market, which required delivering multiple bakery boxes, I had transportation with more style, albeit dated.

A few years back, my mother had turned Gram's 1972 Volkswagen camper van into a food truck. It was pumpkin-orange with white trim. We'd always fondly called it "Bread Loaf" because of the shape of its bay window in the front. Through the years, she had shuttled me to school, summer camp, bonfires on the beach as a teenager, and finally, to college. Now, with a White Squirrel Pretzel sticker on each side, she had a new life ferrying me to the farmer's market each week.

I slid open Bread Loaf's side door. I placed the bakery boxes inside, careful to stack them so that they would not fall. I buckled Mouse into the front seat and then stepped around to the driver's seat, where I sank into the familiar orange plaid fabric of my childhood.

I turned the key, and she rattled to life.

As we drove along Main Street, Mouse hung his head out the window, enjoying the breeze blowing against his ears. He put his head down, though, when I parked at the law office. We were both feeling vulnerable today after what had happened last night. I let out a heavy sigh. I rolled down a few more van windows, picked up a manilla folder containing the lawsuit, and told Mouse to stay. It only took a couple of minutes to give it to Kit's receptionist.

Back inside the van, I reached over to scratch Mouse's chest. He barked as we pulled up to the town square. The salty air was filled with the aroma of kettle corn and barbecue. We could see batik fabrics and silvery wind chimes blowing in the wind. We heard bluegrass music, and in the distance, someone was playing an African drum.

In the middle of the square, farmers sold vegetables, fruits, herbs, olive oils, soaps, and preserves. Food trucks usually found spaces along the street lining the square. I had to cut the wheel hard to back Bread Loaf into a spot across from the library. Mouse sniffed the air as I unbuckled him. He knew the drill. First, we walked around the block in the other direction so he could sniff around and find a place to do his business. Afterward, we walked to the Forgotten Coast Coffee food truck for my latte and for him, a pup cup filled with whipped cream.

Back at the van, with Mouse now satisfied, I got

ready for customers. I opened both of Bread Loaf's massive barn doors on the side and hung burlap twine across the opening. I used clothespins to display clear bags of different flavored soft pretzels. On a card table just outside, I arranged boxes of pretzel bites and different dips. Last, I set out a blackboard easel and used chalk to write today's specials: Oreo-crusted pretzel with cheesecake dip and pepperoni pizza pretzel with marinara.

Early morning is when the farmer's market is busiest, and throngs of people were passing by my food truck. Only a few actually stopped, though. I always offered free samples that usually ran out fast, but today, after what happened with Moriah, people acted afraid to come near my food.

A pale woman in a bucket hat strolled by with two canvas shopping bags loaded with mustard greens. I made eye contact and stepped out from the food truck. "If you like cheesecake and Oreos, then you have to try these little honeys," I said, pushing a plate of sample pretzels in front of her.

She set down her bags and scanned the plate, then looked at the logo on my truck and raised her eyebrows. "I'm surprised they didn't shut you down for food poisoning. Aren't you the same bakery that killed that woman?"

"Okay. First of all, we, I mean, I didn't poison anyone," I said, lowering the plate. I wasn't expecting this. My stomach sank. "The police are investigating, but they don't know how Moriah Moore died. Yes, she had just eaten our dip."

At that, the woman picked up her bags and scurried toward several parked cars along Main Street.

I set the plate on our table and began scratching Mouse's belly. He rolled over. At least one of us didn't care that no one was buying pretzels.

"There you are," said Ana, an artist and dear friend. She was a regular at the farmer's market. She sold beautiful handmade painted pendants and beaded earrings that echoed her native Mexico. She usually left her mother in charge of her booth while she shopped for this week's groceries.

"Hey, lady."

"I brought you something. It's from my new collection," said Ana. "I heard what happened. If you need anything."

"I know, and I would do the same for you," I said. If the town wasn't exactly circling the wagons right now, at least I had enough friends to make a semi-circle. Maybe, too, those friends might have some information that could help my investigation. "Did you interact with Moriah here at the market?"

"I really didn't. She sold her produce when it was in season and those Beet Boxes. Those were really popular, but mostly, she had other people hired to run her booth."

"What about Cal? Was he getting along with her?"

"Like I said, I rarely saw Moriah here, but I can say the few times she was here that Cal treated her well. He even bought some of her Beet Boxes."

"Thanks. If you hear anything else, would you call me?"

"I will. I want to help. My heart breaks for Moriah's family but also your family. That bakery. Its history and the way it's a part of the fabric of this community." She hesitated and then reached for something in her pocket. "Oh, and Casey June, take this for a while, to borrow."

said Ana, producing a dusty blue velvet choker with a very large, ornate silver and turquoise heart-shaped pendant and a simple gold bangle bracelet. "I'm loaning these to a few friends around town to encourage people to talk about my business. When you wear these, do you mind taking a selfie and posting it with the hashtag Ana handcrafted?"

"Of course," I said, pocketing the choker and slipping the bracelet on my wrist.

"Oh, Casey June, are you coming tomorrow to Night Y'all?"

"Night, what?" I asked.

"Night Y'all. It's an event tomorrow night in the square to celebrate National Farmer's Market Week."

"Well, then, yes. I'll see you and all y'all tomorrow night," I said, making her laugh.

As Ana walked away, I saw Carlisle Williams, the attorney who served me papers at the bakery the day Moriah Moore died. She was walking toward me. Like Moriah, Carlisle owned a small organic farm, something she envisioned pursuing full-time when she retired.

I was going to get her attention, but Carlisle reached for her ringing phone.

At the same time, the orange cat walked in front of me as Carlisle passed.

The cat swished its tail in front of Mouse's nose, setting off a riot of barking and growling, and ultimately a bump to a table leg that led to several pretzels falling into the grass below. At that, I decided it was time to pack up Bread Loaf.

Soon, the cat walked away. Mouse stayed close and rubbed his nose on my calf. As I reached down to pet him, he licked my hand.

"I know, I know," I told him. It was time to go find his favorite food truck, Knead More Dog Biscuits. I always got him a peanut butter biscuit when we left the market. You could set your clock by this. Mouse remembered, and he was going to do whatever it took to make sure that I didn't forget.

I folded the chalkboard easel and closed the van's barn doors, then scrambled to leash Mouse before he left without me. We walked to the other end of the square and found the retro turquoise camper where other dogs and their owners stood in line. The same orange cat reclined in the grass, licking its paws. She rolled over so that I could scratch her belly. Mouse panted and salivated, then sat his hind legs on my feet as we were waiting. He ignored the cat and kept his eye on the prize.

"Mouse! How you been, buddy?" said Loomis Bohannan, the owner of Knead More Dog Biscuits, as he walked out to hand Mouse his treat.

After Mouse got his treat, I looked around to notice that I was the last one in line, so I leaned in closer to Loomis and half whispered to him, "Did you know Moriah well?"

"Not really," he said. "Her food, though. Everyone in this town had bought a Beet Box at one time or another."

Just then, a voice from behind me chimed in. "Not me."

I turned to see Sam standing there in his campus police uniform. "What brings you to the farmer's market?"

"Lunch. And I have a weakness for kettle corn." He scratched Mouse between the ears. "The last time I saw you, Mouse wasn't looking too good. Do police have any leads on Moriah's killer?"

"I wish. We're not exactly receiving rave reviews at the Squirrel right now."

"Want to talk about it over lunch?"

"Actually. I can't. I really need to get back to the bakery." There it was again. I felt like my heart was in the air. I knew I was blushing and used Mouse as an excuse to leave sooner. "I have to get him back for his nap."

I turned as quickly as possible and trudged toward the street to find Bread Loaf.

Once we got close, I noticed the orange cat had followed us and was rubbing against my legs.

While all of this was going on, I was walking and fumbling with my keys at the same time. Then, Mouse made a low growl and stopped beside me. I didn't look up until I was right next to the van door.

That's when I saw it.

What should have been an orange plaid interior was now mostly white. There was something in the front seat—a fifty-pound bag of flour had been slashed! A butcher's knife was protruding from King Arthur's chest. Someone had scrawled in thick marker: *You're knot that clever.*

Chapter 4

I called 911 and, while I waited, tried to move some of the flour from the front seat. It was a futile effort. By the time Fin arrived, I was wearing most of it.

He pulled up in his black pickup truck and quietly shut the door. He coolly walked toward me in a checked button-down shirt and faded black jeans.

He stopped, looked down at my shoes, still covered in flour, and sighed.

"I thought you were coming down to the station to answer more questions today," he said as his gaze finally met mine.

"It was on my list. Believe me."

"You didn't disturb any of the other evidence, did you?"

"I left the flour bag. The knife fell to the van floor." I had taken a picture of everything and showed that to Fin.

As we were talking, Sam walked up to see what all the commotion was about. He said he heard the 911 call on the scanner.

Fin refused to meet Sam's eyes or answer any questions. He acted like he was too busy bending over and in and around Bread Loaf looking for evidence. For my part, I was too rattled to say much to Sam. He offered to take Mouse's leash and walk him around the square while I waited.

Crime scene personnel took pictures and carefully removed what was left of the flour still in the bag. The rest would need to be vacuumed.

Fin held up the knife and note in two separate clear plastic bags and spoke to a forensics expert. Then he turned to me. "Did you already have this flour in the van?"

"No, but this is the bag that was missing from my usual delivery this morning at the White Squirrel. I'm not sure if someone took it before I walked out or if they took it before the others were loaded onto the delivery truck."

"I'll need to check security footage at UPS and the bakery," he said.

I dropped my head. *He's not going to like this.*

Fin blew out a deep breath. "Let me guess. You don't have security cameras?"

"We're a centuries-old family bakery in a small town. We worry more about humidity on a sticky Georgia summer afternoon affecting how our dough rises."

After a long pause, Fin offered to drive me home, then warned me about staying out of the investigation. "I heard from Loomis Bohannan and a few others at the farmer's market that you have been asking around about Moriah. I know it's instinct to get involved, Casey June, but please leave it to the professionals, okay?"

Just then, Sam walked up with Mouse, and whether he realized it or not, he strained his relationship with Fin even further by insisting I ride home with him. Sam's hazel, nearly green eyes, seemed to pierce through Fin as he looked him squarely in the face and said, "I've got her."

Fin shook his head and walked away.

****

Back at the White Squirrel, I found Gram sitting with Mouse on the deck. He was getting his fill of key lime pretzel bites, something that probably wasn't going to help his weight problem.

Gram looked up as I approached. "I know. I know," she said. "He shouldn't be eating this, but I can't say no to Mouse."

I sat down next to her and took her hand. "It's okay. We missed you. I'm just glad you're here."

She smiled, and I released her hand. We sat in companionable silence for a few minutes, and then I rose and looked out toward the ocean. "You stay here with Mouse. I think I'll take another short walk."

I didn't tell her I wanted to go back to the original crime scene where Moriah had been found. The lawsuit still weighed heavily on my mind. Was it possible to get to our family home or maybe find a way around? I also felt like I had missed something the night I discovered Moriah's body.

As I walked to the edge of town, I pulled Mom's cardigan around me closer. I inhaled the earthy, woodsy scent of the mossy oaks. Then, up ahead, I saw the gate blocking the roadway. The crime scene tape had been removed, but the "No Trespassing" sign was still there.

The orange cat peered out from the bottom rung of the gate, then rose up to scratch my leg. I leaned to rub her fur when I heard what sounded like someone running toward me. Before I could react, my feet were swept out from underneath my body. I screamed out and fell backward in the sand, grazing the edge of the gate's post.

33

My legs were scratched, and there was a gash on my left ankle. I could only take short breaths as I sat down, dazed, to look at the damage to my legs.

I looked around. No one was there, but I had an eerie feeling I was being watched. I scrambled to my feet and wasted no time getting out of there.

The cat walked with me as I hobbled my way home. I felt sorry for myself more than afraid. It was still light outside, and people were walking back from the beach with strollers and kids in tow, enough activity to make me feel somewhat safe.

Once inside the bakery, I climbed the stairs and opened the apartment door to find Gram doing the crossword at the kitchen table. She took one look at me and dropped what she was doing.

"Oh, June Bug, oh no. Are you okay?"

"Someone just knocked me down. I think I'm just banged up a little." It hit me just then how terrifying the attack had been. I looked down to see the cardigan that I was so proud of had a rip at the hem.

"Did you call the police?"

"No, I want to have time to talk to Sam about what he knows about Moriah. Please don't tell Fin. Not yet."

At this, Gram brought me in for a hug. "Give yourself one day, then you need to tell him, or I will." She released me from her arms and held me back for her eyes to take me in. "I think this is a good night to make Midnight Seafoam. You remember the recipe?"

"How could I forget? I might have been the only girl growing up on the island allowed to drink spiked hot chocolate." I couldn't help smiling and falling back into her warm embrace. We linked arms, and she helped me hobble into the apartment kitchen.

I put the kettle on and grabbed the Irish coffee glasses. She reached into the cabinet for two bottles—white crème de menthe and green crème de menthe. Funny, I hadn't noticed those since moving back into the apartment, but I wasn't entirely surprised. Gram had a way of stocking up on the most impractical provisions.

In a few minutes, she poured boiling water into each glass. She added cocoa, sugar, and the white crème de menthe. She stirred and then nodded when it was time for me to spoon a dollop of whipped cream on each. She muttered something under her breath, but with the throbbing in my head, I didn't pay much attention. Then, she added the finishing touch: a drizzle of the green liqueur on top.

We carried our hot drinks to the couch and arranged a throw blanket over our laps. I leaned my head on Gram's shoulder as she used the remote to turn on the TV and selected a re-run of *Murder, She Wrote*.

For the first time in a long time, it felt good to be home.

****

I tossed back and forth in bed all night. At three o'clock in the morning, I gave up and shuffled to the apartment kitchen in a T-shirt and shorts to start the kettle.

Getting up early has always brought me comfort. I can hear myself think. I can collect my thoughts and listen to my body. Surprisingly, my ankle no longer throbbed from last night's attack. I had bandaged the wound but found today that it, and other scratches on my legs, no longer required covering.

The kettle whistled, and I poured the steaming water over a bag of Earl Grey tea.

I took the mug and crawled back into bed with Mouse and opened my laptop. Mouse lifted his head and peered out briefly, then burrowed deep inside the covers next to me. I wanted to find out more about Moriah's ex-husband, Henry Cherry. I knew he owned several buildings and businesses in town, but other than that, I knew little about him. After typing in his name, I found he owned the 1930s cottage that housed Lucky Beach Nutrition and a handful of other homes now zoned for commercial use along Main Street. He was also the owner of two car washes. There wasn't a lot of other information other than his appearance at the chamber of commerce or charity events.

I searched court records to find that Moriah had filed for divorce last year, but it had not been finalized.

After a quick shower, I styled my hair and tucked it neatly behind one ear. I took a little extra time with my make-up, adding mascara and lipstick for a change. I reached for a cobalt blue cardigan that Mom knitted for me in high school to layer over a powder blue blouse and yoga pants.

I had to tell Sam about last night's attack. I still wasn't ready to tell Fin. I had my reasons, largely because he didn't want me poking around in his investigation.

I reached for my phone on the nightstand and texted Sam.

Me:—*Got plans for breakfast?*—

After a few minutes, my phone dinged.

Sam:—*It's a little early for breakfast. Coffee, though?*—

Me:—*I'll unlock the bakery door. Coffee in five.*—

Downstairs in the bakery, I looked out the window

to see the ocean and sky still dark. I could hear the ebb and flow of the water.

I reached for a small coffeepot I kept behind the counter and plugged it in. I filled it with water and then found the stash of my favorite flavored coffee, Turtles in a Cup. I poured the coffee beans into a small grinder, pulsed it twice, then dumped the contents into the coffeepot. Five minutes later, a buttery pecan, caramel, and chocolate aroma wafted from the kitchen to the front of the bakery.

Sam let himself in, and I motioned him over to the bar where I had set out cream and sugar. I poured two mugs of steaming coffee and sighed, glad to see him.

He was wearing joggers and a T-shirt and clearly had done little more than roll out of bed. He used one hand to rub the right side of his face, which was dark with stubble. He sat on a bar stool next to me and smiled. Our hands bumped into each other as we reached for the mugs, sending a small electric current through my arm.

I looked away for a moment. Then, I came out with it. "I was attacked last night. At the gate that leads to my family's home. I'm okay, but I needed to tell someone."

Sam set his coffee down, his hazel-green eyes wide awake now. "Did you file a report?"

"No, and I haven't told Fin yet." I took a sip of my coffee. "I wanted to ask you about Moriah. Had she gotten into a fight on campus? Did anyone have it out for her?"

"I haven't shared everything up to this point because I didn't have a lot to go on, but if we're going to work together on this, I want to tell you what I know so far," said Sam. He sipped his coffee, then took in a breath and let it out. "We know that a student on campus named

Jessie was disputing a grade."

"Well, we will need to speak with him."

"Her," he corrected. "And you're not going to like this one, but we have reason to believe that Cal was upset with her, too."

"I didn't know that Cal went over to the college. He's so busy with everything else."

"They only knew each other through the farmer's market. He had submitted an application to the market board to sell pre-made meals, but when Moriah found out that her Beet Boxes would have a competitor, she apparently called in a favor from three of the board members, who later rejected Cal's application."

"How did he take that?"

"Well, he continued selling spices from his booth, but he didn't complain to anyone about not being able to sell the pre-made meals," said Sam. "Instead, he was trying to imitate her business online. If you ask me, he had too many irons in the fire."

"Typical Cal. He starts a lot of projects and has a lot of ideas." I stood up and walked behind the counter and pointed to a selection of pretzels in our display case. "Want a little something to go with your coffee?"

Sam smiled, and I took that as a yes.

I began plating two cinnamon-sugar pretzels as he continued speaking. "I'm more interested in that student. Apparently, she changed her major from paralegal to pre-nursing. She had a B in Moriah's ethics course, and it was keeping her from being accepted into the nursing program, which is highly competitive and based on GPA."

"Did you find anything in Moriah's office from the student?"

"No, the police have sealed it off, but when they are done, I will do my own search. The only thing I have is the student's written complaint against Moriah. It's pretty scathing."

After rinsing our mugs in the sink and making Sam a cup of coffee to go, I walked him to the door. He thanked me as we walked out onto the deck together. Then he reached down to touch my forearm. "Be careful."

His hand was toasty and slow to move from my arm. The sensation was like warm honey in my veins. My lips parted, and I took a deep breath. "I will."

Chapter 5

That afternoon in the bakery, I relived all that had happened: the threat left in the van and the attack at the gate. I knew I needed to prepare for tonight's class at the community college, but I wasn't in the right frame of mind. I told Gram I was anxious to the point of jumping out of my own skin. She suggested a nap, but I knew working in the bakery would keep my hands busy and my mind occupied.

Fin texted later that afternoon saying that Bread Loaf had been processed and was cleared as a crime scene. He was having an officer drop her off in an hour.

I looked out from the bakery kitchen to see two customers lingering at a table in the corner; it was almost closing time. Gram was now at the counter, dipping pretzel sticks in chocolate and rolling them in sprinkles.

I moved a tray of blueberry pretzels out of the proofer where they had been rising then to the oven. I added butter, cream cheese, and sugar to my stainless steel mixing bowl and reached for my hand mixer to whip everything together before adding lemon zest.

I put the kettle on the stove while I waited for the pretzels to finish baking. In a few minutes, I was sipping lemon ginger tea and texting Brie:

—*Got class tonight but not feeling it. Not after today. Worried.*—

I set my phone down and looked at the message I

sent. I always waited a few seconds. But there was nothing.

To further take my mind off things, I reached for my phone again and promoted my mystery literature class to my online followers: "Blueberry pretzel meet lemon cheesecake frosting. Come get some on campus tonight."

It was four o'clock already, and I wanted to review notes for the current book that I had assigned to the class. I needed to shower and change. Though bakery life and wearing flour on my shirt had become the norm, at least once a week, I wanted a little of my old life in Atlanta back. Upstairs in the apartment above the bakery, I took the time to style my hair, then neatly tucked it behind one ear. Instead of wearing my go-to cardigan and blouse, I put on a sleeveless black dress that touched my knee at the hem, a recent find at the thrift store. I traded my clogs for some strappy sandals, then walked out to the apartment living room to find Gram reading her favorite Harry Potter book to Mouse, who cocked his head and seemed to listen. They looked to be settled in for the night.

"I'm on my way out. I'm leaving early to set up," I said, leaning down to kiss her.

She squeezed my hand and took off her reading glasses. "Couldn't you cancel after what has happened?"

"I'm scared, but I'm okay."

After grabbing my small leather backpack, I walked downstairs to the bakery and placed the pretzels and dipping sauce in a single bakery box then headed for the door. I usually rode my bike to the college because the entrance to the long and narrow college drive was only two streets from the bakery. It was on an old land grant near Seabrook's forest district.

The light outside was fading as the sunset began showing off a little, mixing with orange and pink clouds. Salty air filled my nose, mixing with the scent of food from diners along Nutwood Street. I looked around warily, then secured the bakery box on my bicycle's pannier rack and pedaled away.

Class started at 6:00 p.m. that night, and I was there about fifteen minutes early. Tonight, we were discussing Agatha Christie's *Death on the Nile*, a personal favorite. I had planned an activity in which students were each assigned a suspect to impersonate so that we could dig deep into character analysis.

Students came in, some even dressed to look like their characters. One brought a fake pocket revolver, and another had gone to great lengths to dress like a 1930s socialite. An hour passed as students gave their presentations and grazed on blueberry lemon pretzels. I wrapped up class by encouraging everyone to attend the writing club on Saturday in the old faculty house on campus.

After class, I lingered to answer questions from a handful of students who stayed behind. They had a literary analysis due in a few weeks.

As I walked across campus, I heard the familiar whine of a scooter. I turned to see Cal on his beloved Vespa. A woman dressed head to toe in black leather with a red silk scarf around her neck was lifting a leg to climb onto the back.

"Gram?"

She smiled mischievously. "We just got out of class, too. We're taking a continuing education class. Piracy and Plunder on the Georgia Coast."

When I didn't respond immediately, my

grandmother cocked her head to one side. "I wanted to get more involved at the college."

For Cal's part, he seemed to be only a sidekick. He looked at me guiltily. "Don't worry, Casey June, I'll have her home by nine o'clock."

By the time I reached my bike, clouds covered the moon, and it was, as they say in Georgia, "as dark as pitch." I didn't like riding in the dark, especially after what happened at the farmer's market, but I knew the sooner I got on with it, the sooner I'd be home, safe and sound. I secured my bag on the panniers and began pedaling as fast as I could through the forest district. At night, the coastal pines overhead felt like they were bearing down on me.

My eyes began to water as I hurried along. Then, headlights were suddenly on me from behind, making me wobble as I rushed to the side of the road.

"You need a ride?" said Sam, from the window of his truck.

My voice cracked as I made one word into nearly three syllables. "Yes."

Sam loaded my bike and turned to me. The scent of his aftershave blended with the night air—a mix of citrus and nutmeg. "After all that's happened, Casey June, I really don't think being out here alone like this is a smart move."

"I know. I guess some of my stubbornness comes from Gram."

Inside his truck, we drove with the windows down. As he moved his arm to shift gears, he reached for a water bottle and grazed the back of my hand. Something told me it wasn't an accident. My heart beat like cool, steady rain.

As we pulled up in front of the White Squirrel, Sam helped me unload my bike.

He then stayed in the driveway until I had unlocked the bakery and turned a light on at the door. I waved goodbye and dead bolted the door, then tiptoed up the stairs to the apartment. I found Gram asleep in my bed, and beside the bed, Mouse was spread-eagle on the papasan chair.

"Really?" I whispered to myself.

I headed for the couch with the spare blankets and pillow, not bothering to change into pajamas. The smell of Sam's aftershave lingered in my mind. I reached for my phone and texted Brie:

—*I might have a crush on my new neighbor.*—

Then, I added:

—*Gram is up to something. I know it.*—

****

The next morning, I woke to the aroma of vanilla and brown sugar. It was a smell I had known since childhood—cinnamon roll pancakes. My grandmother had left a fluffy short stack on a plate in the apartment kitchen with a note. She was already downstairs baking the day's pretzels. I changed into a T-shirt and yoga pants and decided to look for a multi-colored cardigan, one that Mom had knitted for me in high school. Downstairs in the bakery, Gram had already written the special on the chalkboard menu: pecan pie pretzels with caramel dipping sauce.

Cal was at the magnetic poetry board.

They both turned to look at me, and Gram, especially, spent a little bit longer than usual admiring the clothes I had chosen to wear. She smiled as she noticed the cardigan. "We've got it covered this morning, doll. Why don't you take the day off and go do something for yourself? You've been working nonstop since you moved back. Now that I'm here, I can pick up the slack."

I decided what Mouse and I needed was a long walk. I was reliving the threats from the past few days and still feeling rattled. Though I ate the pancakes, I was trying to be healthier, so I popped into Lucky Beach Nutrition for an energy tea to boost my metabolism.

The line was long, and as I stood there peering around at the tables, I saw Fin with a brunette woman about my age whom I didn't recognize. They were sitting outside in a courtyard.

I got my order, a purple and blue tea called Mermaid, and then walked around back, then to the side to keep them in my view. They were laughing and talking. I rolled my eyes, then half pulled Mouse into a bush that bordered the courtyard. I thought I had backed away far enough so that I wouldn't be seen. I looked back up to notice the woman was now sitting alone. I heard footsteps behind me. Then came Fin's deep Southern accent. "Looking for something?"

"Hi, just going for a walk." *And hoping a hole in the ground opens up, so I can crawl in and die.*

"In the bushes?" said Fin, reaching down to pet Mouse, who offered a pre-emptive lick to his hand.

"Well, my dog had to go, you know, do his business."

"Right," said Fin, not buying any of it.

"We really need to go." I tugged at Mouse's leash.

I saw a path leading to a public beach access and took it. Tourists were pulling wagons filled with beach chairs and blankets. The sky was clear, creating an almost turquoise ocean below. Gulls called out as they hovered over the sea foam, and waves gently lapped against the shoreline.

Up ahead, I saw Nissy in front of a mossy oak along the path. She was carrying a basket and was squatting near a splintered birdhouse on the ground. I remembered that faded blue birdhouse usually hung from the tree. It was long abandoned, missing the front wall and leaning to one side. Now it was busted and splintered.

Nissy turned to me, caught a little off guard as I walked up to her. Relief came over her when she recognized it was me and held up an empty envelope. "I thought you might have been the person who has been stealing these."

Nissy had a scavenger hunt, now known throughout Seabrook as The Book Hunt. She created it the same week she launched a YouTube channel encouraging people to "get caught reading" at Lemon Meringue. She also included coffee gift cards to her cafe and bumper stickers that read "My Honors Student Pretends to Study at Lemon Meringue." It was a fun way to promote literacy and encourage people to come to the cafe's weekly "read-ins."

I bent to help her pick up some items in the sand. "What happened?"

"I usually hide two books a week. I add clues online, and winners of The Book Hunt have instructions in each one they find to take a selfie with their new loot and then hashtag Lemon Meringue. This past week, there were no posts. I came out here to see what was going on."

"What if whoever found them just didn't want to post to social media?"

"No, I've been hoodooed. Not only were the gift

cards gone, the books were destroyed."

Most people would be happy to find a gift card and a book. "Who would do something like this?"

"I don't know. Being against reading and coffee is like being against cake and ice cream. They just go together," said Nissy, frowning as she picked up the remaining pieces of a copy of *The Girl on the Train*. She bought used books all year for The Book Hunt. "This one is destroyed."

I helped her collect everything, and we walked further down the beach access until we found a weathered lifeguard chair. We decided that the wooden box built into the chair would be a perfect place to hide the new treasure—a handmade bookmark, gift card, sticker, and a paperback copy of *The Girl with the Dragon Tattoo*. After tucking everything inside and closing the wooden box, we made our way back to the boardwalk. I invited her to walk back to the bakery with me, but Nissy said she had to get back to her cafe. She also had to post a new promo for The Book Hunt, offering clues and letting folks know this week's books had not been found. She planned to repair the birdhouse and hang it back on the tree.

Nissy turned to me to bring me in for a side hug before she left. "How's everything at the Squirrel?"

I shook my head. "I'm going to find out who killed Moriah Moore. I have to save my family's reputation. If I don't, the bakery will not survive. It's all I have left from my mother. And with Mom gone now…"

"What about your grandmother?"

"She just comes with the place," I said, guiltily, thinking how big a role she played in my raising.

We both laughed. Then turned when we heard

someone else laughing.

"Like the white squirrels?" Donna Jean power walked by us in a baggy sweatshirt and joggers. She carried an oversized pink leopard travel mug.

Nissy and I took a beat to absorb what just happened. Had she been listening to our conversation? What was she doing out here anyway?

Donna kept moving and yelled over her shoulder, "Never mind me over here getting my steps in."

Chapter 6

Heading away from Nissy, the next few minutes passed quietly as I walked a little slower back to the bakery. The afternoon sky stretched a limitless clear blue. A crescent moon hung low in the southern sky. Vintage coastal Georgia. As I finally approached the bakery, I found Sam sitting on the porch.

"Hey, you." I pulled my hair out of a ponytail.

A cool breeze blew across my skin. Funny how a good walk can take your mind off things, though I suddenly was aware this wouldn't last long. Whatever he had to say, there was worry written all over his face.

He stood and shifted uncomfortably. "I didn't tell you this, but your grandmother has been coming around the college, meeting people. Some students are in a class with her and Cal."

I let out a heavy sigh. "I know. I saw them both last night on campus. That's what Gram does. She is looking for something to get involved in, though I usually worry about the outcome."

"I'm taking that class with her," he said. "I can take one class a semester tuition-free, and since I'm new to Georgia, I want to learn more about the history of the barrier islands."

"Just be careful what you learn from her," I said, looking down and smiling to myself.

"That's what I wanted to talk to you about. Our

class. She has invited us to tour the bakery later in the week, something about a pirate's ship and gold. Apparently, this house was owned by an ale maker who stole gold from a ship and used a kind of ancient chemistry to turn the ship's crew into…"

He trailed off.

I knew where this was going. "Into white squirrels?"

"Yes."

We both laughed.

I knew the historic home that housed our bakery was one of the few places in town where folks might still see a white squirrel. I also knew that at one time, the island was home to a colony of white squirrels. This and the fact that townspeople kept stories going about our family made for conversation starters at cocktail parties. As fun as it was to believe the story, none of it was true.

"Want some advice? Take little of what Gram says seriously," I said.

While this was the first I'd heard of the class tour of the bakery, I knew enough about Gram to know that these were mostly just stories. And she loved an audience.

I smiled and looked down. My grandmother was not one to run things by me first. She lived in the moment.

After Sam left, I found my phone and texted Brie:

—*Need you here. This new guy… Don't know that I want to start anything. Don't know if I want to stop it either.*—

By three o'clock that afternoon, I just had a couple of bakery customers lingering at tables. I went out to the front to refill coffee mugs and offer to-go boxes. Soon the customers were gone. I took off my White Squirrel Pretzel apron and was getting ready to turn the light out when my grandmother walked through with two trays of Irish crosses. The pretzels were twisted and formed into the shape of palm-sized crucifixes. She was getting ready to store them in containers. "These are for my classmates and professor later in the week," said Gram.

She began to tell me all about it when I waved my hand. "I know. From Sam."

"I knew you wouldn't mind." She raised one eyebrow and smiled in a self-satisfied way.

I simply kissed her cheek and started up the stairs to the apartment. I had a lot going on tonight. First, there was an event on the square called Night Y'all to celebrate National Farmer's Market Week. I knew that a lot of the town would be at that event, and I wanted to find out more about Moriah Moore's life and her ex-husband. Then, later in the evening, I planned to honor my obligation to lead our community writing club, The Back Porch.

I changed into a White Squirrel Pretzel T-shirt and a black cardigan. I wanted to take samples of our pretzel bites to promote the bakery at Night Y'all. I decided against taking my bike after the attack, so I loaded Bread Loaf, pointed her in the right direction, and revved the engine.

The event was little more than a banner across the entrance to the town square, a guitar player and folk singer, and of course, local farmers and other businesses promoting their goods and services. It was kind of like a Chamber After Hours under the starry sky. I walked over to a table loaded with Lucky Beach protein bars and ordered the largest energy tea they had. It came with a sticker on the cup that promised me it would be a pick-me-up and would stimulate fat burning. I was still feeling puny from the attack, dehydrated from all my walking, and of course, guilty from all the food Gram had been making.

I set up the card table I kept in the back of Bread Loaf, then offered pretzel bite samples. Normally, I came out to events like this to promote the bakery and talk business with other people in town. Tonight, though, I wanted to talk to as many people as I could about Moriah.

A couple in their mid-fifties strolled by. They were a little sunburned and wore matching Seabrook T-shirts, so I guessed they might be tourists. They took a pretzel bite from the table, but I couldn't exactly pump them for information on Moriah.

After they left, I spotted Donna Jean holding court at her table. A crowd had gathered. She was offering Queen Bean souvenir Mason jars. The jars came with cold brew coffee or iced tea. Donna began telling the group something, then pointed so that they looked at my table. She gave a friend-enemy wave, and I countered with a "bless your heart" smile.

Soon, a man and his daughter came to my table. The girl had her eye on one of my cinnamon-sugar pretzel bites. I used tongs to add it and cream cheese dipping sauce to a white paper bag when the man looked down at my shirt.

"Isn't your bakery the one accused of food poisoning?"

I handed the bag to him before I could answer. He accepted it reluctantly and walked away.

That was pretty much how the night continued.

As the evening wore on and foot traffic slowed, I spotted Carlisle Williams, Moriah's law partner. Her pixie hair was always spikey, but tonight, it had unusually stiff peaks. She had a farmer's market canvas bag on one shoulder with two bottles of wine poking out. Under her other arm, she carried a painting by a local artist.

I rushed to her side. "Carlisle. I'm Casey June Hart. I don't know if you remember me."

She looked down and then back up. "I know who you are."

I pushed the tray of pretzel bites in front of her. "I just had a few questions about Moriah. I know how difficult all of this must be for you. Did you know anyone who wanted to hurt her?"

"No, I don't," she bristled, pushing back the tray. "I'm gluten-free, so thanks, but no thanks."

"Why was she out by the gate leading to my family's home that night?" I looked down to see the orange cat swishing in between her legs.

Carlisle was clearly agitated by the cat and took a step back. "That was just Moriah. Always thorough. She wanted to make sure staff had posted the No Trespassing signs. It was the last thing on her list before she headed home for the evening."

"Did anyone else know she was driving out there?" My stomach churned.

"Only a few people at the law office and her husband, Henry Cherry. He stopped by that afternoon. They met in her office, and he lingered too long, if you ask me. She got rid of him by telling him she needed to drive out there."

I listened and shifted my feet from side to side. *She seemed overly eager now to share information. Why?* I told myself to play it cool, which was becoming increasingly hard to do. My injured ankle was beginning to speak to me. Though it had felt better earlier, it was now a constant throb. And thanks to that bucket of mermaid tea, I needed to use the restroom. "Do you know why he wanted to talk to her in the first place?"

"They had filed for divorce a year ago but retained joint ownership of some of the businesses and properties they owned. I think he was just being nosy as usual." Carlisle's face hardened. "He was controlling. He liked to know where she was and what she was doing."

****

Later, as the event winded down, I packed up my things and headed for Bread Loaf. The orange cat kept pace with me, stopping here and there to rub her tail against a lamppost or arch her back on my calf. I stopped to scratch her ears and realized she wanted to go with me. I opened Bread Loaf's doors, and she leaped into the passenger seat and began licking her front paw.

I drove down the road in silence, listening to the night air. A firepit glowed in the distance, the faint ghost of burned marshmallows blended with the salty air. Back at the bakery apartment, I changed into shorts and a T-shirt and checked my hair. I decided it was time to text Fin:

—*I need to tell you something tonight. Busy?*—

Fin:—*Just finished at the gym. I'll stop by on my way home.*—

Me:—*I'm downstairs in the bakery. Door's open.*—

Then, I walked into the bakery looking for a corkscrew for a bottle of wine. I also checked my hair a second time with my phone camera.

One glass of wine and thirty minutes later, I was playing with the magnetic poetry wall when Fin walked into the bakery. He was his usual cool self. He wore a dark gray button-down shirt and blue jeans. He must have just showered at the gym because his hair was wet and filled the air between us with lime and cedarwood. He ran his hand through it, and I felt like my heart was being held under a wave.

I looked down, embarrassed, then motioned for him to sit at the counter. I didn't want him to think this was a date, and at the same time, I didn't want to be treated like his little sister anymore. "What'll it be?" I pointed to the chalkboard menu above. "Today's special was ham and gruyere with slaw and pickled onions on a pretzel bun."

Fin met my gaze and smiled in a way that said he was proud of me and also admired me. He looked tired. "I'll have the ham sandwich. Make it regular cheese."

"Coming right up."

I turned toward the kitchen and sliced two pretzel buns, then prepped two sandwiches, his with American cheese and mine with gruyere. I laid a quarter slice of dill pickle on each plate and brought them out with strawberry lemonade and a dessert plate piled with my newest pretzel bite: raspberry streusel.

Fin looked down at his plate. His warm chocolate eyes lit up. "You know me too well." He took a bite of his sandwich and chewed slowly. He looked back up into my eyes, then got serious. "What's on your mind? I know you didn't just have me over to the bakery for taste testing."

I hesitated but knew I had to tell him. "I was attacked last night. I had walked back to the gate leading to the lightkeeper's house. I don't know what I was thinking. I guess I was looking for something."

"Were you hurt?" Fin widened his eyes.

"Just scratched up. I'm okay, really, but I wanted you to know."

"I don't want you investigating, Casey June," said Fin, now in detective mode.

Are you kidding? "What do you expect me to do?" Each of my breaths felt smaller and more restricted. "The bakery's reputation has suffered. The investigation has been slow. It's affecting my business. Most of the town thinks I had something to do with Moriah's death."

Fin had by now finished his sandwich. He thanked me then, as he turned to leave, pinned me with a hard stare. "It's hard to do my job when you're always getting hurt or I have to worry about you."

"It's not your job to worry about me." I folded my arms.

"Please. Let me handle this." He clenched his jaw. "There's a lot about the investigation that you don't know."

"I know that every day I wait for the police to solve this case that I lose more business," I said, immediately regretting the insult.

"Let me remind you that you're still a suspect." Fin stormed out without letting me get another word in.

He slammed the bakery door.

I let out a small yelp and bit my lip. I shouted in my best Liz Lemon voice, "Another successful interaction with a man!"

Then, I did what I usually did when I was at my wit's end. I turned to Brie:

—Why has he always been like that? Fin is the worst when it comes to being strong-willed. He still treats me like some kid sister.—

Later that evening, I knew prepping food would take

my mind off Fin. I would be heading soon to The Back Porch, our town's writing group. They needed something to go with what was usually a terrible cup of coffee.

I decided to try a twist on an old family recipe for pretzel balls. These were basically small rolls, hollowed out and filled with beer cheese. I usually liked to bring the group something sweet, though. So I skipped the cheese and filled each one with raspberry preserves.

When I had a sheet pan of twenty-four prepared, I melted a bar of dark chocolate and coconut oil in a double boiler, then dipped the pretzel balls into the chocolate.

While these cooled on wax paper, I noticed Hazel at the bakery kitchen window. I grabbed a piece of the leftover bread, the part that I had hollowed out, and walked outside. I lay the bread on the ground near my feet, and Hazel followed.

I looked her in the eye. "What if Henry Cherry followed Moriah out to the gate that night? But where did he get a Carolina Reaper? And why did she have my jalapeno dip with her?"

After a long silence, I left Hazel, and instead of climbing the stairs to the apartment to change, I grabbed one of Gram's cardigans from the coat rack. It was oatmeal in color, and the cotton rag style dressed up my T-shirt and shorts. I turned around in it and felt less stuffy and a little more like I was going to meet a group of real writers, not some of the pretentious wannabes I used to find myself with in Atlanta.

With all that was going on, I opted to take Bread Loaf again. I loaded the bakery box in the back of the van and drove to the college.

The Back Porch met once a month in the old faculty

house on campus. It was a log building dating to the 1920s, built in a lodge pole style with open rafters and no walls except for the restrooms and a small kitchen.

Sam was already standing in the kitchen with Nissy when I got there. They had just put the coffee on. I set out the chocolate-covered pretzel balls on a tray, and we walked out to the main room to find most of the group already assembled at the few tables and chairs in front of the fireplace.

The Back Porch was an odd collection of townspeople from different walks of life, young and old. Some had aspirations of writing a novel of their own. Others wanted to solve real-life mysteries and were interested in true crime stories. There were a few who, in keeping with small towns everywhere, just wanted to keep up with what's going on and who's doing what. I would have put Corrine, our town librarian, in that group.

Our regular members also included some college students; Roy Bryce, the weekly newspaper editor and his wife, Evelyn; and some residents of the assisted living facility nearby. This was Sam Shore's first meeting.

Tonight, the group was supposed to be discussing *The Lady Sherlock Series*. On a projector screen, someone had posted something about internal conflict and external conflict. But Corrine had already commandeered a dry-erase board and a marker. She wrote Moriah Moore's name in red at the top of the board.

"Who are the most likely suspects?" Corrine asked the group.

"Her husband," said Nissy.

"What about her law partner, uh, what's her name,

Carter?" said Roy, looking to his wife for approval.

"Carlisle," said Sam.

My obligation was to lead their discussions each week, so I tried to turn the conversation back to writing, but I was also interested in finding out as much as I could about Moriah.

Corrine, though, who accused nearly everyone of damaging books when they returned them to the library, added little to what I already knew.

After meeting for an hour, we had managed to accuse nearly everyone who lived in Seabrook. Not that I was upset to see Donna Jean's name on the list, but it was ridiculous. However, we agreed as a group to stay in touch as we pieced the case together, and I felt like my semi-circle of support was growing just a little.

Afterward, I volunteered to stay behind with Sam and lock up. We put the folding chairs away and unplugged the coffeepot. I boxed the leftover pretzels and gave them to him to take home.

Sam smiled and pointed to the door. "I'll walk out with you."

I liked the gesture. I was feeling paranoid after the attack.

He walked me to the van and offered to follow me home, but I declined. I needed to be alone.

I drove home and took Mouse out to the mossy oaks in the backyard where we watched two white squirrels scurry up a silvery tree trunk. I looked in on Gram, who was sitting at the small apartment kitchen table, reading about pirate ships and Georgia's colonial history.

I wrapped myself in a silver chenille throw and walked out to the bakery deck and down to the beach. There was a full moon tonight, and the tide had just gone out. I stood at the water's edge for what seemed like an hour, then wandered a little further down the beach, stopping as I noticed loggerhead turtles coming up from the ocean to bury their eggs in the sand. I sat so as not to disturb them and watched in silent bliss.

I loved this time of year growing up. As a child, my mother would wake me in the middle of the night and hand me a flashlight so we could find our way along the boardwalk. We would turn our lights off when our feet hit the sand and walk quietly along the beach. She would spread a quilt below us and hold me in her lap, wrapped in her thick shawl. We would watch the turtles, and she would whisper tales of our ancestors in my ear.

Years later, in high school, I had come out on nights like this with Brie and Cal. We volunteered with the Sea Turtle Patrol to mark turtle nests with tiny orange flags so no one disturbed the eggs. Occasionally, a nest had to be moved because it was below the high tide line.

Both Brie and Cal had decided our senior year that they wanted to be veterinarians. I wanted to be a writer and had contemplated staying in Seabrook. The thought of being left behind in our hometown scared me, so I followed them both to Savannah College. Those first two years in college were blissful, but after Cal and I broke up and Brie went missing, I moved to Atlanta to be closer to another man I was dating. I felt like I was running away.

Now, sitting by myself in the sand, a flood of memories came over me. While I had been busy running away from my hometown, following another boyfriend to numb the pain of Brie's disappearance, I wasn't in Seabrook when Mom passed away.

My mom had been kayaking along a series of sea

caves and got caught in a high tide. Gram saw her go under, but the authorities never recovered her body. The kayak was later found washed up on the rocky shoreline.

I wiped hot tears from my cheeks and reached for my phone. I texted Brie:

—*I should have been here.*—

Chapter 7

The next morning, my alarm went off at five o'clock. Half asleep, I pushed the covers back and slid off the side. Two books on the bed—last night's reading—hit the floor with a thud.

I shuffled into the kitchen to start the kettle and found Mouse curled up on the rug next to the dishwasher.

I turned the kettle off, pouring glorious steaming water over green jasmine tea. I wrapped myself in one of my mother's scrap quilts and walked down to the bakery and out to the deck, breathing in salty air. The ocean was unusually quiet this morning. I sat in one of the cafe chairs, propping my feet on the table and looking down to marvel at the scraps of fabric cut into shapes of crescent moons and stars and pieced together. She had made this quilt decades ago when she was a new mother, much younger than I was now.

I took a generous sip of my hot tea when the orange cat cleared my leg to land on the table in front of me and then climbed down to sit on my lap. I rubbed her head against the folds of the quilt. I brought her in close to my chest, and she purred.

After finishing my tea, I had an idea. I carried the cat inside and tiptoed back up the apartment stairs. She jumped from my arms and sauntered into the kitchen. I had the sense that she knew the place. She rubbed against an old terra-cotta pot where we grew mint. I thought about giving the cat some of Mouse's food, then I thought of something else. I opened the freezer, grabbed a Lean Cuisine, and popped it in the microwave. In a few minutes, the cat hunkered over a black plastic tray, lapping up brown gravy and tearing apart herb-roasted chicken.

Afterward, licking her paws, she looked up at me. Sunlight was filtering inside, and it made her yellow eyes flicker. Her motor was running, and she was getting drowsy. I smoothed the fur on her back.

"I think it's official. You belong here, Lean Cuisine," I told her. "Hope you don't mind me calling you that. Also, I hope you don't mind sharing a bed with a warm beagle."

I carried my mug to the papasan chair that had been in the apartment since the 1960s, spread the quilt over my legs, and reached for my laptop on the nightstand.

I was committed to proving to Fin and the town that I wasn't a killer.

I began searching the internet for more on Henry Cherry. What kind of relationship did he have with the businesses that leased his buildings? What had taken so long to finalize his divorce with Moriah?

Gram came into my room and raised her eyebrows. Lean Cuisine was now sleeping above me on the papasan cushion. Mouse was wedged into my side.

"I knew it wouldn't be long. If you hadn't brought that cat inside, I would have," she said, peering down at my laptop. "Research?"

I didn't want Gram to know that Sam and I had been looking into Henry Cherry. Cherry was on the board of regents at the college, and I knew how Gram was. I trusted her, but I didn't need her to go all frontier justice or Robin Hood on me.

I knew it was time to talk about the bakery, though.

I was worried about the White Squirrel before Moriah was killed, but now, I was terrified that the only thing my mother ever loved could go under. Also, I had to tell her about the lawsuit.

"I'm looking for ideas, a way to throw an event to increase business at the White Squirrel. I am worried, Gram. We usually have a full house at breakfast and lunch, but this past week, we could count the number of customers each day on one hand."

"What about pitching the bakery as the venue for this year's college fund-raiser? I have been volunteering at the foundation office on campus once a week before our night class meets. It's folding papers and stuffing envelopes mostly, but I'm becoming kind of an insider. I learned last week that the country club was the original site but had to back out because of a norovirus outbreak."

I swear she winked at me when she said those last words.

She continued, "The annual fund-raiser is usually hosted by one of the country clubs. Kind of a good ol' boy network, if you ask me. It's time one of the small businesses here in the downtown has a shot at it."

"Do you really think they would have it here? We could show Seabrook that what happened to Moriah had nothing to do with us. I could work on signature cocktails and come up with new pretzels, dips, and sandwiches."

"You type up the proposal. I'll make sure it lands on the college president's desk." She moved in closer to touch my face.

"Gram, there's something else." My stomach sank.

"What?"

"That No Trespassing sign at the gate to our home, Donna is suing to block us from using the road."

"I know, honey. I found out the first night back. I'm not afraid of her." Gram waved her hand dismissively.

She walked over to the papasan and climbed in with me and the animal family.

Lean Cuisine, eyes still closed, leaned her head on one outstretched paw above us. Mouse snored happily in my lap. Gram kissed my forehead. "I'm moving back to the lightkeeper's house. These first few days have been great, but this apartment is not big enough for both of us."

"But Gram, we're okay here together."

She stood firmly and kissed my cheek this time, whispering, "I want to give you your space. Besides, the lightkeeper's house is my home."

She walked to the bedroom door and turned. "It's going to be beautiful today. I'll take the morning shift in the bakery. Why don't you get out and enjoy, take Mouse for another walk?"

"Thank you, Gram. I love you."

"I love you."

After she left, I got back on the internet, searching for ideas for the college fund-raiser. A Pinterest webpage showed colorful cocktails. That's when it hit me. The White Squirrel was at the edge of the forest district, nestled among the coastal pines, and the alley behind the bakery led to the state forest. We could throw a "Cocktails and Trails" event, starting guests at the bakery's deck under twinkle lights and serving pretzel finger foods like sliders and bratzels and drinks in sweet little Mason jars. Then, guests would move along the forest trail for other cocktail and food stations as well as games and auction items. The night would culminate in a bonfire at the end of the trail.

I scanned the college website to see if they had tentatively placed the fund-raiser on the calendar. It was set for next Wednesday. March 29. I froze. *The tenth anniversary of Brie's disappearance.*

I reached for my phone and instinctively started texting Brie. I erased it several times before deciding on just:

—Come home, B.—

****

Two hours later, I finished typing the proposal for the Cocktails and Trails event. I printed it and left it on the kitchen countertop in an envelope next to Gram's favorite tea—cinnamon sunset.

After a shower and changing into a well-worn T-shirt and leggings, I put Mouse on his leash and decided we would walk farther today, to the dog park. I decided to use his retractable leash because he liked to pull, so much so that he usually coughed and choked as we walked to the park and back.

I made a new mug of tea and wanted to enjoy it before going, but Mouse whined again, so I decided I would take my mug with me. I slipped into my clogs and grabbed a jacket and out the door we went.

We made it no further than the corner of our bakery when Mouse noticed a white squirrel next to a city trashcan enjoying the result of someone's bad aim. A small paper basket of sweet potato fries lay strewn on the sidewalk. Mouse barked. The squirrel rose up and froze. Then Mouse jerked without warning. Hot tea spilled out of my mug and onto my forearm, and I dropped his leash.

"Mouse! Mouse! No. No. *No!*"

Mouse ran at full speed and crossed the street at Covington. The squirrel was nowhere in sight.

I ran and ran, but running in socks and clogs is like being wrapped in cotton. I was shuffling, mostly. I caught a glimpse of Mouse as he stopped to sniff something important. Then, in a flash, he was off again, running back down Covington as hard as he could go. For both our sakes, Covington dead-ended into the park.

I continued to yell. This caught the attention of one neighbor, who also yelled. Then, two motorists pulled over at the same time. One car, the nearest to me, had an open window.

The driver yelled, "Get in!"

On impulse, I opened the door and got in the car. The platinum blonde woman behind the wheel stepped on the gas before my door was even shut. She turned to me as she shifted into second gear. "We have to save that baby!"

Hot tears filled my eyes. If I had had any courage left after losing my mother and worrying now that her much-loved bakery was going under, it was now running down my face and onto my shirt.

The woman driving pulled her black sunglasses down the curve of her nose to look over at me. "Honey, I'm Lindy Knuckles," she said, using her freshly manicured, candy-apple red fingernails to pluck a pack of tissues from her black leather bag and hand it to me. "I work at the Christian rock radio station. Don't worry. I've done this a million times. My schnauzers are always getting loose."

She looked out the driver's window as I scanned the passenger side. With each empty yard we passed, my heart sank.

We drove through alleys behind beach houses and got out to walk and call for Mouse.

An hour later, I was heartbroken as Lindy drove slowly back around to the bakery.

I let out a deep breath and managed to thank her as I got out of her car.

"I'm so sorry," Lindy said in a nasally voice.

I skulked back inside the bakery, hoping no one would see me. I didn't have the heart to tell Gram what had happened. After the threats this week to Mouse's life and my own, here I was, being careless enough to lose him on my own. I felt two inches tall.

I sank into my couch and tipped over to the side. I must have fallen asleep.

I woke a few hours later on a tear and snot-stained throw pillow. My phone was ringing. It was a doctor's office near the town square. They had found Mouse and his retractable leash tangled in a thicket near the bark park.

****

I cleaned myself up and claimed my dog who, upon seeing me, looked like the guilty pup he was for running off and causing so much worry. We made up quick, though. After licking my chin and sitting on my feet while I thanked the medical staff, we both trudged to where I had parked Bread Loaf. We climbed in and clattered home.

I called the doctor's office later to ask if I could bring lunch to their staff as a thank you, to which they said, "Yes." I also contacted the radio station to tell Lindy the good news.

Before I could get a word in, she tried to soothe me.

"We have been praying on the radio for Mouse."

"Well, it must have worked. A doctor and her staff found him this morning. I just went to pick him up. I am making lunch for them. Can I bring you lunch, too?"

"I'd love that," said Lindy. "You know what, let me come by the bakery to get it. Besides, I want to see that baby now that he's home."

Later that afternoon, I joined Gram in the bakery kitchen. She said there had only been four customers all day. We had also reached the limit on our credit and were now having trouble getting deliveries for the bakery.

As she was talking, I looked down at my phone to see a voice mail message from Kit Westmoreland, the attorney. He had agreed to take our case and fight the lawsuit, but the retainer was $3,000.

"What is it?" Gram asked.

"Nothing."

I sighed and began, as usual, to focus on food. I could always lose myself in coming up with new ideas in the kitchen, so I began making hero-worthy lunches for the medical staff and Lindy as promised.

I toasted two pretzel slider buns, then spread fig jam between each and added bacon and brie cheese before toasting a second time. I put each sandwich in a pastry box and placed a cup of fresh fruit inside as well.

I drove Bread Loaf to the doctor's office and delivered the lunches.

When I returned, Mouse was ready for a walk. I was still feeling raw from what had happened earlier, so I put a harness on him to help with his pulling. I also wrapped his leash around my arm twice and held on tight.

When we returned, I found Lindy pacing outside on the sidewalk next to the bakery deck. She was on her phone. When she saw us walk out, she quickly put it away.

"Hey there," she said, squatting to Mouse's level.

"I'll be right back," I said, rushing into the bakery to get her lunch.

When I returned, she was gently tugging one of his ears. "I'm glad you're behaving."

"He pretends he is." I handed her the pastry box with a thank you note on top. "I hope you're hungry. You have no idea how grateful…"

Before I could finish the sentence, though, hot tears filled my eyes. I felt my knees buckle, and I half wobbled to a bench on the sidewalk.

"Is everything okay?" Lindy put a hand on my shoulder. "Listen, I can tell when someone is hurting. This is more than Mouse getting off his leash this morning."

I dug my sandal in the sand below the bench. "I'm just working through some things right now. Really, I'm trying to figure out what to do next. It's no secret that our bakery has been struggling, and now with Moriah's murder, people have stopped coming in. I was already teaching a night class to help pay some of our expenses. To top it off, I am being sued, and I don't know where I'm going to find the money."

"Why don't you come down to the station?" she said. "We need someone in the afternoon, anyway. We just had a girl leave for college, so we need a receptionist. We also need help on Saturdays during our call-in show."

I could only nod my head in agreement. I couldn't even mumble an answer. This had been a roller coaster of an emotional day.

Lindy smiled. "You can bring Mouse, and if you don't, I will hold it against you."

Finally, I drew in a deep breath. "I'd love that."

"You know, Moriah's husband, Henry, owns the radio station," Lindy said.

"I knew he owned a lot of businesses in town and commercial real estate, but I didn't know he was into radio," I said. *This part-time job may lead to more than extra money*, I thought.

"Do you know if Henry had anything unusual going on recently? Like a fight with Moriah?"

"No, sorry. I didn't know her, but he comes into the station a lot, keeps an office there, and has a room that is off-limits with his personal files." Lindy tapped a finger on her chin.

Chapter 8

By the time Lindy left, it was late afternoon, and Gram had closed the bakery. I noticed Sam's truck was in his driveway. I needed a distraction from my money problems, and this new information about Henry had me wondering. With that many businesses in town, shouldn't he be doing very well? Why had he bothered Moriah about her family's money?

I texted Sam:

—*Got time to eat a raspberry cheesecake pretzel?*—
Sam:—*Only if coffee is involved.*—

Me:—*I have new information about Henry Cherry.*—

In a few minutes, Sam was walking in the bakery front door, wearing what I would call his "off-duty" clothes: faded gray T-shirt, tight black jeans, and, of course, cowboy boots.

"I brought my laptop. There's a lot these days you can find out about a person on the internet," he said. "I don't have access to everything that the city police do, but I have an advantage over them. I worked as a reporter after college. I know how to look for people, and I know how to dig." Sam held the laptop up to show a database called Accurint.

Soon, he was using what he had learned in his old days as a newspaper reporter to do a background search on Henry Cherry. He typed in Henry's name and the state of Georgia. With the click of a button, we could see everything—property taxes, how long he lived at different addresses, speeding tickets, even turning up a newspaper article for an open house five years ago for the Christian radio station. The article listed Henry and Moriah as owners.

A more recent article reported that Henry had made some bad investments, and some of the businesses he owned had become debt-heavy and would file for bankruptcy and not be paying creditors.

"Looks like he doesn't even live in Seabrook," Sam said, his fingertips gliding over the keyboard as he typed. "They list his address here as Jekyll Island. Looks like he keeps an office at the art gallery he owns there, too."

"That's about twelve miles away."

"Road trip?"

****

After Sam left, I climbed into bed with Mouse and Lean Cuisine.

I filled Brie in on everything:

—I have had a day. Mouse got loose. I think the only other day I cried more was the day you went missing. Everything happened today. Attorney called back. It's going to be expensive to fight Donna.—

A few seconds lapsed.

Then, I added:

—I'm trying to turn things around here at the Squirrel. I sent a proposal to the college to host their annual fund-raiser. Fingers crossed. I'm picking up part-time work at the radio station.—

Me:*—On the road tomorrow with Sam. I think we're on to something. Moriah's ex-husband owed a lot of money, and he would have needed her family's money to* *bail him out again.—*

I waited a few seconds.

Me:—*Oh and Sam's cowboy boots are getting to me. In a good way!—*

For the first time since Moriah's death, I was feeling just a little upbeat.

****

The next morning, I was still eating Cheerios in my underwear when my phone dinged.

It was Sam. He was already downstairs.

I took a few extra minutes to get my stick-straight brown hair to hold beachy waves, then headed for Mom's closet. I skipped the yoga pants and opted to pair one of her sleeveless blouses with a casual cotton skirt that touched my knee.

I was wearing sandals that showed off my pedicure as I padded down the spiral staircase and into the bakery.

In the kitchen, Gram was busy prepping the specials for the day. I had already filled her in on everything. Inside the bakery kitchen, the smell of pretzels filled the air. She was pulling the first of four trays of ham and cheese breakfast pretzel rolls from the oven when I kissed her on the cheek and squeezed her hand.

"Are you sure you can manage without me?" I asked, feeling guilty for leaving for the day.

Cal walked between Sam and me as he pushed a cart with two bulk bags of flour. I was not sure he had said a word to Sam since Sam had moved to town, and I was certain that Cal didn't like Sam being my friend. He turned away from me and said, "We got this, don't we, Icy Faye?"

I'm not sure who I worried about leaving the bakery with for the day more—my grandmother or Cal.

Together, though, they made a good team.

After looking back at the two of them a second time, I headed out the door as Sam held it open for me. Outside, it was the start of another beautiful day. The air felt cool and light on my skin. I could hear children laughing on the beach. There were couples holding hands, walking along the sand.

When we got to Sam's truck, he walked around to the passenger side and held the door for me.

"Thanks. You don't have to do that, though," I said.

"I'm from Kentucky. I think I do," said Sam, smiling.

Inside his vehicle, he turned to me. "Any requests for road food?"

"Well, I'm trying to be a little more healthy. What about Lucky Beach Nutrition? I'm kind of hooked on their energy teas," I said.

"That sounds great."

A few minutes later, we were sipping day-glow yellow, purple, and blue teas with names like Beach Bum and Mermaid and enjoying the view along the coastal highway and swapping life stories.

I told Sam about my life in Atlanta, teaching English, attending writer's critiques, eating brunch, and ordering twenty-five-dollar bottomless mimosas.

Sam told me about Kentucky and being raised on a horse farm. He had recently gotten divorced and took the job in Seabrook to make a fresh start.

Ten minutes and half an energy tea later, we were on Jekyll Island. We turned off the main road and parked in front of a small shopping center that housed a yoga studio, gift shop, some offices, and Henry Cherry's art gallery.

In the early morning heat, we got out of Sam's SUV to smell the first funnel cakes of the day being made at a parking lot food stall. As we walked to the far end of a touristy stucco shopping center painted a beachy turquoise and pink, I spotted the art gallery and noticed through the windows that there were two people inside. We went in and pretended to look at kitschy painted plates and driftwood wall panels. We overheard a man who looked to be in his late sixties tell a woman about a piece of art she had ordered.

"It simply hasn't come in yet," said the man, who stroked his thick white furrowed brows.

The woman left in a huff, rolling up the sleeves to her Jekyll Island sweatshirt. After she left, Sam and I reluctantly approached him.

"Excuse me, I am Casey June Hart, and this is Sam Shore. We live in Seabrook, and we wanted to pay our condolences to Moriah Moore's husband. Does he work here?"

"I'm Henry Cherry, but we, Moriah and I, were technically still married when she passed, but it's no secret that we were getting a divorce." He looked down for a second, then sighed. "But thank you for coming all this way. Is there something else I can help you with?"

Sam decided to come out with it. "We know that you came to see Moriah at her law office a few hours before she was found dead. Did that have something to do with needing money from her?"

At that, Henry's face turned red. He hurried to the front door and held it open. "I think it's time for you to leave," he said. "Casey June, I know who your family is. I know Seabrook is a small town and filled with gossips, but I never expected this from someone like you. If you speak another word about me or my family, you'll be hearing from my lawyer."

"But…" The palms of my hands dripped with sweat.

"And if you step foot on any of my properties again, I'll take out a restraining order!"

Sam put his hand on the small of my back as we headed out the door.

Afterward, when we had time to exhale in the parking lot, Sam and I were incredulous.

"Well, that was a dumpster fire," I said.

Sam raised his eyebrows and blew out a breath. "I guess we should get out of here."

We walked along the shopping center sidewalk to his truck.

A few steps before reaching the truck doors, though, I spotted a weakness of mine, a sweet little food truck selling coffee.

"Yes, but first, some caffeine? My treat this time," I insisted.

Sam smiled and followed my lead. He was picking up on my quirks and what made me tick.

We walked up to the Beachy Bean, a twenty-four-hour food truck, to find flavors like Southern pecan and hazelnut. The barista was a fresh-faced twenty-something and had a nose ring and a tattoo of Frieda Kahlo on her bicep. She told us she was making the special of the day: a German chocolate-flavored coffee plus coconut creamer and salted caramel syrup.

"Basically, it's a slice of cake you can drink," she said.

"I have to have it," I told her.

Sam surveyed the menu hanging under a string of white lights. Then, he turned to me. "I'm looking for something like the coffee you served the other morning. It tasted like caramel, pecans, and chocolate."

That's when the barista cut him off. "Turtle Love?"

When Sam didn't respond right away, she added, "It's hard to describe, but you know it when you find it."

"That...I think that works for me," Sam said. It was the first time I had seen him nervous. There was definitely something in the air.

With our drinks in hand, we turned to leave and began walking back down the shopping center sidewalk. There were a few sale racks outside, and we rummaged through a few of them, laughing at touristy T-shirts, just taking our time.

Soon, we were walking toward Sam's truck. As we got closer, I noticed something brown and goopy dripping down the side.

Sam took his sunglasses off. "Is that?"

"Tiny peanut butter cups?"

Someone had smeared a very thick peanut butter cup frappe down the driver's door.

When we were finally standing within inches of the sticky mess, we saw that someone had written with their finger: *You can't crust him.*

I took a picture with my phone and knew Fin had to be notified.

I bit my lip as I texted the picture to him. I simply wrote:

—*Well, this happened.*—

In a few seconds, he was typing a response:

—*I'm in the area. Stay put.*—

Me:—*How do you know where we are?*—

Fin:—*It could be the Purple Cow in the background that gave you away.*—

78

I looked to the right of the parked truck to see the bovine statue standing in front of the Purple Cow Bakery, a niche business beloved by those in Jekyll and the towns ringing the island.

I sighed. *Nothing gets past Fin.*

Five minutes later, Sam and I had finished our coffees and were contemplating whether to cross the street for donuts at The Purple Cow when Fin pulled up beside us. By then, most of what had been dripping down Sam's door was on the asphalt.

Fin got out wearing gray jeans and a button-down blue plaid shirt. He walked around to where Sam sat with the driver's side window down. There wasn't much to see. "Are you sure that this doesn't have something to do with not tipping your barista?"

I sighed and pulled out my phone. "You saw the photo. Someone knew we were here and must have followed us or watched us."

Chapter 9

Fin wrote down our statements and said he would use the photo on my phone to file his report. He hardly looked at Sam while he was there.

After I watched Fin's truck pull away, Sam and I climbed back into his truck.

I looked down at my now-empty coffee and sighed.

"You realize that we've only had tea and coffee since leaving this morning." I cut my gaze to the sign next to the Purple Cow proclaiming it was Kolaches Tuesday. Their barbecue brisket and Cheddar-stuffed sweet pastry was legendary.

Sam forced a tired smile. "Lunch?"

"I thought you would never ask," I said.

Inside The Purple Cow, we pigged out on a plate of kolaches. I kept running through my mind who would have known we were on Jekyll Island this morning. "Did you tell anyone about our trip?"

"No." He leaned back in his seat. "Did you?"

"Only Gram and Cal. Unless they told someone, or at the bakery, a lot of people overhear things," I said.

We finished eating and used the drive home to discuss Henry and Moriah. If he did really need money, why not sell one of his businesses? Did he need something else from her, too?

****

Later, after Sam dropped me off, I walked around to

the back door of the bakery to let myself in. As I opened the door, Lean Cuisine bolted out. I watched her trail off in the distance but didn't have the energy to chase after her. She'd be back. It had been a long day. Inside, the bakery kitchen was empty, and I could hear a few voices out front. I saw Gram cleaning tables. Cal was folding pastry boxes. The light outside was fading.

I tiptoed up the spiral staircase in the hall.

In the apartment, I found Mouse fast asleep on the couch. Someone had wrapped him in a throw quilt.

On the kitchen counter, there was an envelope from the college and a pastry box. On the box, Gram had scribbled something in her sloppy handwriting: *Make sure you're eating.* I raised my eyebrows. If only she knew. In fact, I had been eating very well, too well, by the way my skirt gripped my waist.

I opened the envelope first. It was a letter from the college's foundation chair agreeing to rent the White Squirrel Pretzel for $4,000 for the evening of the fund-raiser. They would pay $3,000 for food. There was a check for a total of $7,000. They would settle the tab for the open bar after the event. After expenses, I estimated that we would have enough to pay the lawyer's retainer and some left over to pay at least two overdue bills. That was a start.

I kissed the check and spun in my socks across the hardwood floor.

Next, I opened the pastry box that Gram had left for me. Inside, there were two pretzel bun sliders with Nashville hot chicken and pickles and a side of coleslaw. I walked the box to my bedroom and sank into the papasan, feeling grateful and a little unworthy of Gram taking such good care of me. As I ate, I checked my phone for any updates on Moriah's funeral. I checked the Seabrook Voice and read an article about an Art Auction and Wine Pull in honor of the late Moriah Moore.

It seems there was a private burial planned for family only, so friends of Moriah's had organized the art and wine walk to raise money for a charity that was dear to Moriah's heart, the Good Karma Pet Rescue. Several galleries and some other businesses agreed to display a number of pieces by local artists. A silent auction was planned. Along the many stops, people could also pull a random bottle of wine from a wall and make a charitable donation.

The art and wine walk started at 6:00 at Watermelon Creek Tasting Room, a small wine bar owned by Brie's parents, Blake and Meg Kidwell. After the event kicked off there, people could walk to several galleries, a bank, the chamber of commerce, and finally back to the tasting room's patio to dedicate a garden with repurposed artwork in Moriah's memory.

I checked the time. It was 5:00. I had enough time to shower and change and narrowly avoid Gram's gathering of about fifteen students and her professor downstairs in the bakery.

I texted Nissy.

Me: —*Are you in the mood for art and wine?*—

Nissy:—*Only if I can drink while I look at the art! Are you going to the art and wine walk?*—

Me:—*Yes!*

Nissy:—*Does that mean I have to get all gussied up?*—

Me:—*Yes! I'll meet you there.*—

I opened my closet. I had few options for occasions that called for dressy. I was going to wear the same dress as the other night and accessorize it to look a little different. I decided to layer the dress with a black shawl, another piece of clothing from my mother. I tied it in the front and then turned the shawl to the side so that the tie was on my shoulder and the shawl fell at an angle across my thigh and midsection. I pulled on black tights and a pair of black suede ankle boots that I had not returned to Nissy.

I finished drying my hair and tucked it behind one ear. Then, looking at myself in all black, I decided I needed some color to pull my look together. I remembered Ana's dusty blue velvet choker and fastened it around my neck. The pendant—a turquoise and silver sacred heart—rested on my collarbone. Perfect. I looked folk chic enough to pass for the art crowd, if not a level or two above a box wine drinker.

I took a selfie and posted it online with the hashtag Ana handcrafted.

I sent the photo to Brie and a message:

—I'm going to a memorial tonight for Moriah. Wish me luck on getting any information.—

I also wanted to get the word out about the upcoming Cocktails and Trails event. I used my computer to create a flyer and printed copies, then descended the stairs into the bakery. I walked to the front counter and noticed Gram had arranged a few trays of pretzels for her class, along with a pitcher of sweet tea.

I used tongs to prepare a pastry box of pretzels to take to the art and wine walk. After closing the box and setting the flyers on top, I looked out to see Gram sitting on the deck outside. She held a mug and seemed to be talking to someone, though no one was around.

I walked out to find her rubbing Lean Cuisine's

belly.

"We're just catching up," she said.

When I said nothing, she added, "Long day?"

"The longest," I said, bending to scratch Lean Cuisine, too. "She must be good at listening because I sometimes talk to her, too."

"You know, I was feeding this cat before I went out of town."

"You mean *went to* prison?"

Gram didn't even look up, then added, "I worried about her, especially since she's never been a cat before."

"Who?"

"I think you know," she said with a twinkle in her eye.

"Gram, I don't believe in your stories. You've got to stop doing this. Please tell me you won't be telling tales tonight to your classmates and professor. That our ancestors used this house to lure the crew of a pirate ship, then cast a spell to turn them into white squirrels."

Without answering, Gram reached for a book next to her on the table and gave it to me. "I've been wanting to give this to you since I returned. I guess now is as good a time as any."

I turned it over in my hands, *A Mergirl's Guide to Backyard Witchery.*

The hard cover was dusty green. The title had black lettering that had faded, though the author's name still shone in gold leaf: Oakley Carolina Craig, my mom. It was written before she had married my father.

I shoved the book in my bag and frowned. Was she trying to make me cry? Was she trying to make me worry about her sanity? Because she was succeeding at both.

Gram looked at me pleadingly. "I was with your mother that day out at the sea caves. We packed a picnic and ate, and I helped her carefully port the kayak down the rocks to the water. Of course, I wasn't going exploring with her. I had brought a book to read, and I was content on the quilt. Once out on the water, she waved."

Lean Cuisine leaped into her lap as she continued telling the story. "I walked a little among the sand and rocks. I had not been to that area of the island since I was a girl. I wasn't gone more than forty minutes, but when I returned, the surf had picked up, and the tide was coming in. I didn't think anything of it. My Oakley had always been tougher than any boy. I raised her that way. I went back to my book, then I heard a strangled voice calling intermittently as waves crashed onto the rocks.

"That's when I did it," said Gram, trembling now. She sucked in a deep breath. "I pictured the orange tabby I had as a girl, and I uttered the spell over and over as poor Oakley surfaced again and again. I was paralyzed with fear. At my age, I couldn't swim in strong surf like that anymore, but I could save her another way."

Fat tears swelled in my eyes, and a river began to run down my face.

Gram was crying, too. "I howled that spell at the ocean until I had no voice. Until there was nothing but water and roar and an empty kayak bobbing against the rocks. I dialed 911 and bawled like a baby as I told the operator our location. Soon after, I must have fallen. I don't remember anything after that. The sheriff's deputies found me and decided that they couldn't safely look for Oakley that night. They took me home."

Gram stroked Lean Cuisine's belly. "I woke the next

morning at the lightkeeper's house and walked out to find this little honey.

"It's her," said Gram, pointedly. "Whether you want to believe it or not, I turned your mother into a cat to save her."

"*And* Hazel and the other white squirrels are the crew of a pirate ship. I know."

Gram stood up to hug me, and I pushed her away, feeling shame and embarrassment.

I walked across the deck, feeling the weight of the book in my bag. Lean Cuisine brushed past me.

Inside the bakery, I reached for my pastry box and flyers on the counter. Some of Gram's classmates were starting to trickle in. Sam was one of them. Another student, a town councilwoman I recognized as Georgia Green, had already picked up one of the flyers.

"I'll be sure word gets out," she said. "Are you staying for our discussion?"

"No, I am going to the art and wine walk for Moriah."

"Oh, many people don't know this, but one of the biggest dilemmas Moriah faced was battling her law partner over a side business they created together," said Georgia, wrinkling her nose. "Something called Beet Boxes."

Chapter 10

I decided to walk to Watermelon Creek Tasting Room. It was a balmy evening with a mild breeze. The sun had just gone down, leaving pink and orange hues along the horizon. I was walking away from the coastal forest district and toward the town square, but I could still smell the longleaf pine and cypress swamp mixing with the salty air.

After my conversation with Gram, I was looking forward to Nissy and her very ordinary life. Read: normal parents, grandparents who lived in another state, siblings, a business that wasn't under investigation. You know, the typical trappings of small-town life.

I turned the corner onto Main Street and found Nissy sitting on Watermelon Creek's porch couch swing. She had traded her T-shirt and jeans for a sleeveless, dark purple blouse, black skinny jeans, and flats. Her wavy, strawberry-blonde hair was up in a bun with a single chopstick. One loose ringlet at her temple floated in the wind.

Nissy had divorced about two years ago and was trying to get back out there and be noticed. By the way she looked tonight, she had a pretty good chance of it.

She saw me walking up. "CJ! Look at you."

"Back at ya. Someone cleans up good," I said.

I tried to hide the fact that I had just had an unsettling conversation with Gram, but Nissy knew something was up. In some non-verbal way, though, she also knew to leave it alone. For now.

I noticed Fin's truck parked on the street. Was he here to interview Moriah's friends and clients?

As we stepped inside the tasting room, I spotted Moriah's husband from the corner of my eye. Henry was talking to the town mayor and some other people in suits who I didn't know. I waved at Brie's parents, Blake and Meg Kidwell, who were busy pouring wine.

Several people were crowded around bar tables and chairs. Others were more curious about the art that had been donated and were milling around. There was a framed portrait of Moriah displayed on a table in the middle of it all. I walked over to sign a guest book. I scanned the signatures to see who else was there.

I remembered the flyers for Cocktails and Trails and reached into my bag.

Nissy leaned closer. "Don't look now, but here comes Donna Jean."

Donna was a few feet from us and was opening her mouth to say something. But before she could get a word out, Nissy had snatched a flyer from my hand and had given it to Donna. "Hope you can make it," said Nissy, using the announcement of the Squirrel's event as a kind of hush puppy for our friend-enemy.

It worked. Donna walked away with a strained look. A lot of downtown businesses would have loved to have hosted the college fund-raiser.

Afterward, Nissy snatched the entire stack of flyers from me, minus one, then leaned in.

"That's her younger sister," said Nissy in a hushed voice, pointing her head to the bar where a thin woman stood with long, wavey hair so blonde it could have been the color of snow at sunset. She wore a black jersey A-line dress and played with a chartreuse scarf around her neck.

I recognized her from Lucky Beach. She worked weekdays when I ducked in for my usual, a purple and blue energy tea. I told myself the teas helped to keep cravings at bay, but I really just loved the colors and sweet and sour taste.

I wanted to talk to her before folks left for the next stop, and this was my chance, so I walked over with the remaining flyer.

"I'm Casey June Hart," I said, realizing that I didn't want to give too much information about where I worked since that was likely where Moriah's last meal had come from. "I didn't know Moriah well, but she was a part of the community."

"I see you every morning at Lucky Beach. Mermaid tea, right?"

"Yes, I'm afraid I may be addicted to those energy teas," I said.

"I'm Jenna—Moriah's younger sister. This event would have meant a lot to her. She loved animals, and her dream was to retire one day and go full-time producer at the farmer's market. We started sharing a city garden plot five years ago, and it just clicked with her. She loved working in the dirt and was proud the few Saturdays of the year when we sold vegetables."

Here's my chance. I have to ask. "Have you heard anything more about what happened to your sister?"

"That kind of pepper is grown only in South Carolina. Moriah frequents the farmer's market here and when she travels, but she's severely allergic to nightshades, especially peppers with any heat. She never would have put that pepper in her food."

"Do you know anyone who knew about that allergy and wanted to hurt her?" My stance grew wider as I leaned toward her.

"No, only family knew. Of course, her husband and possibly her law partner. What's her name? Carlton?"

"Carlisle."

"Yes, Carlisle. She had wanted to be in business with Moriah, making those pre-made meals. Carlisle was making Moriah batty." Jenna took a step back and studied me.

"Can we talk more, maybe later this week? My number is at the bottom of this flyer," I said. "And you're invited to Cocktails and Trails. If you love farm-to-table food, then this event will—"

Before I could finish, she cut me off.

"Hold on," Jenna's eyes widened. "You're that girl. You work at the White Squirrel."

I saw that as my cue to leave.

To make matters worse, Fin looked over from across the room and raised his eyebrows. He knew I wasn't just there to pay my respects to the dead.

I fidgeted with the velvet choker around my neck and noticed most people had already pulled wine from a wall on the far right. Some had written down bids on items for the silent auction. They were starting to leave for the next stop along the art walk, the gallery next door.

I saw Carlisle heading for the door, and I walked out behind her. I reached down to readjust what I had decided was a much too fussy shawl, only to notice Lean Cuisine sauntering up.

"What brings you out here?" I cooed, then thinking

about what Gram told me earlier, I recoiled. I didn't want to fuel Gram's fantasy. It was cruel, too, to think of my mother's death as nothing more than a cliche, made-for-TV reincarnation.

Carlisle turned around, thinking I was talking to her.

"What do you mean? She was my law partner. I had to come," said Carlisle, who was dressed in a powder blue pantsuit. A string of pearls hung from her neck.

Lean Cuisine inched between us and hissed.

"I don't like cats," said Carlisle.

This woman was becoming harder to like by the minute. Gluten. Now, cats. Did she like anything? She was trying to turn away, but I decided I needed to ask about Henry while I had her attention. "I found out today that Henry needed money from Moriah, but why couldn't he just sell a business? Was there something else he wanted, too?"

"Moriah was going to get half of everything when the divorce was final." Carlisle rolled her eyes. "This made Henry furious. Her family money, though, because it was part of a trust and not in her name, couldn't be touched by him."

I texted Fin to tell him I had something important to tell him.

Fin:—*Where are you?*—

Me:—*Still at Watermelon Creek. I stayed behind when everyone left. Guess I'm not fancy enough to bid on art anyway.*—

Fin:—*Almost time for the garden dedication behind Watermelon Creek. Everyone should be heading back there soon. I have something important to tell you, too. I'll meet you in the garden.*

****

The garden had long been planted in the courtyard. Today, in honor of Moriah, repurposed artwork had been placed among the cosmos, marigolds, and sweet peas. The garden had been recreated with twinkle lights, wrought-iron gates, a pair of angel wings, upcycled soda cans and wine bottles, a windmill, and other delicate metal lawn sculptures.

At the entrance, an arbor held a sign that declared it to be "Moriah's Garden of Peace."

I walked to the garden and sat down on a park bench. Nearby, a beautiful girl with long hair the color of honey was twirling under the twinkling lights. I guessed her to be middle school age. She wore a royal blue T-shirt dress and white sneakers.

She snapped a selfie next to the angel wings, then sat down next to me.

"I'm Shea," she said.

"Well, I'm Casey June. My family makes pretzels in town. Nice to meet you."

"I love fairy gardens. This is a fairy garden for grown-ups, though, like an angel garden. The woman this garden is for, Moriah, she needed an angel. She's dead."

I was sucking in air, trying to figure out what to say next and where this conversation was headed.

Out of the corner of my eye, I noticed that Fin had arrived and was walking toward us.

I stood up. "What was it you wanted to tell ..."

Before I could finish, the girl on the bench came running.

"Daddy!"

Fin scooped her up in his arms. For the first time since high school, I saw his serious, no-nonsense face break into a toothsome grin that was ear to ear.

"Casey June," said Fin, now beaming at the little girl. "This is my sun, my moon, and my stars. My daughter, Shea Hatteras Westmoreland."

Chapter 11

Fin flashed a broad smile as he sat down on the park bench and motioned me and Shea to sit on each side. He looked from his daughter to me. Then, he bowed his head as he told a story about how much his daughter and her best friend at school reminded him of me and Brie when we played with him and his brother.

"Remember swimming to the sandbar and burying Kit up to his ears?" he said.

"And dangling sand crabs in his hair?" I grabbed onto his arm.

We both laughed.

He seemed so relaxed. "It's so good. Tonight. You meeting Shea. Everything," said Fin, landing hard on each word, making them stick.

We looked up to see a large crowd gathering at the front of the garden. With everyone back at Watermelon Creek, it was time to dedicate Watermelon Creek's garden in Moriah's memory.

Shea took off when she saw a friend from school.

Then, Fin and I stood for a beat to look for a seat further away from the crowd. We settled on a wicker loveseat near a fire table at the back. We had just taken our seats as the mayor and others gathered up front to make official the Moriah Moore fairy garden for children and children at heart.

Fin put his arm around me, and the coolness of his

touch made me feel like I was in deep water unable to surface. He looked at my lips and smiled, then his eyes brightened. "You said you had something to tell me?"

I sighed, lost in the moment, then remembered. "I think you should speak to Moriah's sister. She knows that Moriah's law partner, Carlisle, wanted to be a part of those pre-made meals. The Bean Boxes."

"Beet Boxes," said Fin. "She was selling them at our gym. She would come in once a week to stock our refrigerator. Take orders. That kind of thing. For people who don't cook and need help with portion control, they were lifesavers."

"Also, Moriah hadn't finalized her divorce from Henry Cherry. I am trying to find out what businesses they owned together and whether he needed money for any of them. What else did he need from her so badly?"

At this, Fin held up his hand. "Stop," he said. "Please let me handle this. I don't want to see you hurt." He looked down, then turned to me. "You know, it's getting late. Let me drive you home."

I didn't feel like pressing further, besides I had experienced a somewhat enchanted evening in the garden with Shea. I didn't want to ruin the moment.

Soon, Shea walked up to take Fin's hand.

The three of us walked to the exit. I reached for the door as Fin reached for it, too. Our hands touched briefly. His hand was like cool water splashing my arm, reminding me of swimming under the moonlight when we were in high school. I drank that in for a beat. Slowly, a smile came to my face.

As we walked out, I noticed a shiny, spotless red truck parked next to Fin's truck.

Sam stood in front of the truck.

Oh, no, I thought, *here we go again. These two.*

I was glad to see Sam, but I couldn't understand why Fin was so hard on him. Or why he insisted Sam stay out of the investigation. Sam was, after all, head of campus police and worked closely with Moriah.

I watched as Fin noticed Sam and shook his head.

For my part, I didn't want to shut Sam out. He never discouraged me from asking questions. Besides, when I was around him, I felt a rush of energy. Admittedly, I felt something similar for Fin, but neither of them had asked me out.

"Sam," I said, walking to stand next to him. "I thought you were at the bakery tonight with Gram and her tales of pirate lore."

"We just wrapped up, and I saw that you were still out here, so I thought I would look in."

This made me feel a little uncomfortable.

Sam looked down at his phone and then back up to meet my eyes.

"Oh, that. I have an app. A few of us do at the mystery writers' group. It lets friends see where each other are at. Your grandmother was kind enough to let me use her phone to get your information, you know, since you're on the same plan."

"You're tracking me?"

"Well, when you put it like that, it sounds like stalking," he said. "I really just wanted to catch up to see if you spoke to anyone tonight, any new leads."

Fin held back as long as he could, but with this, he drew the line. He clenched his jaw and looked directly at Sam. "Listen. I'm only going to say this once. Leave Casey June alone. No tracking. No following. And leave this investigation to professionals. This is not a matter for campus police or some mystery writers' group. If I have to say it a second time, I won't be using words."

I couldn't just stand there and let Fin lash out at Sam like that. "Well, he is a professional. I've been working with him on the case, and we are only asking questions. He's trying to help me and Gram save the White Squirrel."

Fin turned to open the truck door for his daughter, who climbed inside with an "oh no you didn't" look on her face. Then, he turned to me and Sam. "What you've been doing is becoming a target for threats. You've been attacked. You could have been killed."

With this, heat burned behind my eyelids. I looked him down and back up and threw out a reluctant compromise. "We'll stick to what we usually do at our mystery writers' club meetings. We'll look at similarities to other historic crimes, both fiction and nonfiction, and if we ask a few questions along the way, so what? You can't deny us that."

Fin clenched his fists, red in the face. He didn't say another word. He opened his door, climbed inside, slammed it shut, and sped off.

I stood there with Sam, bewildered.

He rocked back on his boot heels. "So, I guess you need a ride?"

****

I climbed into the truck with Sam. We rode in silence for a beat before we both started in, talking over each other.

"What were you thinking?" I asked.

"What do you mean?"

"All of it. Tracking me, following me. You parked next to Fin's truck." I threw my hands up in the air.

"I don't care whether I park next to Fin's truck or not, but it sure sounds like you do." His last words came out with a slight growl.

"What's that supposed to mean?"

"Did you used to date him or something? He seems to put a vibe out to everyone in this town that you are off-limits." He clenched his teeth.

"It's complicated," I said, cupping my forehead with the palm of my hand. "We grew up together. He's Fin. He's like a brother. He doesn't want to see me hurt."

We drove a little further in silence. When we turned onto Nutwood Street, I asked Sam to pull over.

"I need to check the Book Hunt. For Nissy," I said. "I'll be right back."

I got out at the path that leads to the birdhouse and lifeguard chair. Using my phone flashlight, I walked a short distance and checked on both. Each location still had a book, a gift card, and stickers. The loot had not been found, but it hadn't been destroyed either.

Back in Sam's truck, I felt relief knowing that I was just a few minutes away from my pajamas, the current book I was reading, and snuggles with Mouse.

Sam looked over with tired eyes. "Everything good with the birdhouse and lifeguard chair?"

"For now," I said.

"What about us? We good?"

I smiled. "We're good."

After driving just a block more, we pulled into Sam's driveway next to the bakery. He offered to walk with me, but I declined. It had been such a long night. I was ready to head in and lock up.

I said goodbye and walked over to the bakery front porch to see Lean Cuisine for the second time tonight.

"Hey there," I said, reaching down to pet her.

I reached for the doorknob but found the door already gaping open.

The cat creeped in first.

I reached to turn on the light and found everything in chaos. Tables and chairs had been thrown over. Pretzels had been taken from the display case and strewn on the floor. Pictures were broken, and glass was everywhere.

Chapter 12

I called 911. I knew Sam was just one house over, but his lights were already off. I looked up to the apartment windows where Gram was sleeping and didn't see any lights on.

I stood for what seemed like an eternity on the front steps with my thumb hovering over my 911 button, ready to tap it again if whoever did this came running out. Things seemed to be moving too quickly to fully process. *Could someone really still be in there?*

Fortunately, the officers arrived in minutes, including Fin. The sound of their sirens blasted my ears as I stood there numb to it all, their vehicles speeding down the street and their flashing lights illuminating the darkness around me.

I nodded to Fin as he ran up the front steps. He reached for my hand as we walked through the front door. I wasn't prepared for what waited for me inside. Tables and chairs had been thrown over. Pretzels had been taken from the display case and strewn on the floor. Pictures were broken, and glass was everywhere.

There was a warning on the magnetic poetry wall: *Why did the pretzel file a police report? She was assaulted. Leave it alone.*

First one tear rolled down my cheek, then another. After that, I was blubbering. It was all too much after a long day. I was worried about the bakery. Gram's suggestion about the cat.

My knees buckled, and before I knew it, I was on the floor.

Fin helped me to one of the tables and got me a glass of water.

"I'll make some tea," he said.

I folded my arms in front of me on the table and put my head down.

In a few minutes, Fin brought over two steaming mugs. "Do you take cream or sugar?"

"No," I whimpered. I looked up toward the display case and wiped my wet face. Two pretzels were left. "But I'd really love it if you brought over those bourbon chocolate cheesecake pretzels."

Fin put the pretzels on a plate and placed it in front of me. He gave me a fork, but I picked one up and began to make a mess with my hands.

I started to cry a little more. "Who was that woman at Lucky Beach that I saw you talking to?"

"Oh, Marilu, she has been a big help to me," said Fin, knitting his eyebrows.

"Well, it looked like she was helping to make you laugh."

"Casey June, that's not…It's not what you think. She is my father's cousin. She moved in after her divorce. She helps me with Shea after school."

Fin looked down, continuing, "It's been hard since Shea's mother passed away."

"I'm sorry. I didn't know," I said, feeling about two inches tall. *That was horrible of me to say*, I thought.

We began to talk a little about Shea's mother. He said she was someone he met in college. They were just dating. That Shea had not been planned. They were young and scared. When Shea was born, though, she was their whole world.

I knew that Fin's family was helping with Shea. His parents took her one weekend a month so he could catch a break, and they could spoil their granddaughter. I asked Fin about Shea's mother's family, but he seemed guarded on the subject.

Neither one of us said a word for a while, then I tried to change the subject just a little. I tried to relate the best I could by talking about my own childhood and being raised by a single parent.

I reached out to touch his hand. I talked about being raised by Mom and how Gram stepped in when my father passed away. I didn't have a man in my life growing up, a father figure. We both laughed, remembering how protective Fin was of me in high school.

"Why were you so protective?"

Fin clenched his jaw and swallowed hard before saying, "Promise me you'll be careful. I don't know what I would do …"

He didn't finish the rest of that sentence.

Gram rushed into the room and frantically looked around, her face showing relief as she laid eyes on me and rushed toward me. Gram said she heard the police sirens, and it had taken her some time to find her robe before coming downstairs. Though most of the mess had been cleaned up, our front display case was now empty, and there were two trashcans full of pretzels. "What in tarnation?"

I stood up to hug her, then told her what happened. "I came back and found the bakery door open. Someone must have broken in after you closed and went to bed."

"Are you hurt? Was anything taken?" Her eyes

bulged out slightly, and she pinched the skin under her throat.

"No. I don't think so. It was like they just wanted to scare me."

While Fin and I talked, the first responders, under Gram's direction, helped put tables and chairs back in place. Someone was sweeping the remaining pretzels from the floor. After taking a picture of the magnetic poetry board, a crime scene investigator pulled down the threatening verse. They were all helping to clean up, even though they knew they didn't have to.

I cried a little more. *Only in a small town*, I thought.

An hour later, the last of the first responders had left, and Fin headed for the door. He turned around and smiled before heading out. Gram locked the door behind him and hugged me again.

I noticed that Fin did not eat that second bourbon chocolate cheesecake pretzel. I took it with me upstairs. Gram gave me another squeeze before heading to the couch for the night. I kicked off my shoes and shuffled into my bedroom, still wearing my shawl, and sank onto my bed next to Mouse, who was snoring and snorting on one of the pillows. Lean Cuisine was curled up at the foot of my bed.

After setting my plate down carefully next to Mouse, I placed my bag on the nightstand. I unwrapped myself from the shawl and slipped out of my clothes. That's when I noticed the choker around my neck was missing the pendant. I found the T-shirt I slept in and slid next to Mouse. I began to eat the pretzel, one messy, glorious bite at a time.

Two bites in, I reached for my bag and dug out the dusty green book. *Mergirl? Backyard Witchery? Who was my mother, really?*

I texted Brie:

—What do you know about Mom? Wasn't one of your aunts her best friend growing up?—

No response, as usual. I just liked knowing I was still including her. She would always be a part of my life.

I sent one more text and dumped it all out on her:

—What am I going to do with Gram? And this spell book? Is it even possible? I am looking at the feline fur child purring next to me right now. Could it even be? Mom? Oh, by the way, someone broke into the bakery. There was a threat. People in town still think I killed Moriah. I've been eating non-stop. Never mind me over here eating my weight in bourbon pretzels. Been crying. Thinking, too. Fin, he is like sweet summer rain. Then, there's Sam, who I swear is like atomic fireball candy in my veins. What would you do? B, it'll be ten years this week. Remember? Finals were over. Everything seemed possible. You vanished into the night. I'll never give up, though. You'll see on Wednesday. It's going to be a big day for me. I'm going to host an incredible evening for the college, show the town that the Squirrel still has that old magic, and remind everyone that you're still missing. I promise I'll make you proud.—

I put my phone on the nightstand and picked up Mom's book. There were spells for using herbs and, of course, (eye roll) making dough rise. I flipped to a few other pages that had to do with making sachets for love and happiness. There was a tea for healing. *Well, that's good,* I thought. One spell had to do with crystals, positive vibes, and a blessing bowl. *Okay.* Another was for making an enemy love you. *Well,* I thought, *I could use that one in a small town.* Toward the end of the book, though, the spells became a little less J.K. Rowling and a little more Stephen King. Some were for keeping away dark energy and warding off spirits. The words changed from health and spirituality to words like undead and the afterworld.

I drifted off to sleep as I read a spell about bringing someone's spirit back from the other side. It listed ingredients like candles, witch hazel, animal bones, and a handwritten letter. There were instructions to create an outdoor altar on a flat rock. Casting the spell would require the four elements: wind, earth, fire, and water.

My eyelids became heavier and heavier until I sank into a dream. I was walking barefoot along the forest district trail at night. I was following a woman with long brown hair. She was wearing a very long and loose, hooded cardigan around her tank top and faded Levis. The cardigan was gooseberry-colored, and the chunky hand-knitting gave it away almost instantly. *Mom?* But she didn't stop. She seemed to be lost in a dream herself.

Chapter 13

I slept hard and heavy all night. Blame it on the bourbon in the pretzel or just pure exhaustion or worry, but I woke from a deep sleep feeling still very heavy-lidded but rested. It was only 4:00 a.m., and I couldn't go back to sleep.

I relived yesterday's events in my mind. I was still upset with Gram. I was embarrassed by the way Fin and Sam treated each other. I shuddered at the thought of someone breaking into the Squirrel. I had to find out who had threatened me. Someone didn't want me asking questions about Moriah. But why?

Today, though, I was worried a little less about the bakery's bills and the lawsuit keeping us from our historic home. I was thinking about the Cocktails and Trails event. I knew the next day was going to be a big day. For all of us.

As I moved to get out of bed, Mouse popped up and licked my shins. I scooped him into my arms and cuddled him. I noticed Lean Cuisine sitting in the papasan chair, her eyes casting a disdainful glare on both of us.

I attempted to lift Mouse from the bed to the floor, but he resisted.

After showering upstairs, I changed into a tank top and one of Mom's sari skirts, the color of which can only be described as a Moroccan spice market. It had varying shades of turmeric and paprika.

Downstairs in the bakery, I remembered Shea from the previous night, and so I twirled in the kitchen as I started the ovens.

I decided today's special would be Mom's cranberry pecan magic pretzel bites. After making the dough and letting it rise, I rolled out dough balls on four sheet pans. I put those into the oven for a few minutes. Then, after letting them cool, I sprinkled the pretzel bites with shredded coconut, cranberries, dark chocolate chips, and white chocolate chips. The magic was in the next step: drizzling condensed milk over the top, then baking them for another twenty minutes until everything was bubbly and golden brown.

The bakery smelled like toasted coconut, chocolate, and buttery popcorn.

I was putting the first gooey bite into my mouth when Gram came down with Mouse.

"Morning," I said.

Gram muttered "morning" and shuffled past with Mouse, who needed out. She was dressed head to toe in deep purple. No black. She was as beautiful as ever with her silver ringlets tamed into a side braid that rested on her shoulder, but she had lost some of the wind in her sails.

There was definitely a strangeness between us.

I could tell Gram felt rejected. I had pushed her away. But I didn't know if I was ready to make nice.

Soon after, Lean Cuisine sauntered in. She spurned me with another look before sashaying casually to the front window.

By six o'clock, Cal came in, and after composing the poem for the day, he started wiping down tables.

I walked over. "Hey, you."

"Hey, Casey June. I heard what happened last night. Are you okay?"

"Yes and no. I guess," I said. "No one was hurt, but the Squirrel took a beating. Pretzels everywhere. Pictures on the walls were broken. Fortunately, nothing was stolen. We had enough pretzels and bratzels stored in containers in the back to restock the display case this morning."

By mid-morning, only one customer had come in and bought a pretzel breakfast sandwich. *This is not good.* Cal and Gram were drinking coffee at the bar.

I was in the back going over several lists for the Cocktails and Trails event, and was beginning to feel overwhelmed. I had put a lot of pressure on myself to please the college with our venue. I had also planned to use this event to promote our business. The weight of the ten-year disappearance of my childhood best friend seemed to increase with each passing hour. Though not advertised as part of the evening, I planned to remember Brie tomorrow and try to renew interest in her case. I hoped that townspeople would eventually start a new fund to search for her again.

I went through the shopping lists for sliders, decorations, and cocktails. I realized I would have to start now if I was going to make all the stops on those lists. This was also my afternoon to work at the radio station, then go to The Back Porch to meet with the writers' group.

I stared at the lists and broke down, my anxiety climbing and climbing. After a deep yoga breath and swallowing my pride, I poured a cup of coffee and walked out to where Gram and Cal were sitting.

"I need help," I said, laying down the shopping lists

and the menu, which included 500 pretzel sliders.

"We know. We were just waiting for you to ask," said Gram, who glanced at Cal.

Cal looked around at the empty bakery. "Let's close for the day and get to work. That's a lot of slider buns to make."

****

While Gram and Cal worked in the bakery, I took the list of items we needed for the drink stations and headed to the liquor store to pick up the spirits and mixers for our signature cocktails. When I returned, I had just enough time to feed and water Mouse, then make Lean Cuisine, well, a Lean Cuisine, before finally heading over to the radio station to start my first shift.

The day was humid, but with sunshine overhead, I decided it was a great day to head out on my bike. Besides, I needed to check on Nissy's two book hunt locations. I cruised onto the path leading to the birdhouse and lifeguard chair. I got off and walked my bike along. Everything looked in order, so I kept going.

I then headed toward the radio station.

I tried to focus on everything that made our small coastal town so special. The mossy oak tree-lined streets. Shopkeepers sweeping sand from porches. The beach in the distance was full of tourists. Soon, I was cruising into the station parking lot. I saw Henry Cherry walking out of the building. He noticed and walked over as I got off my bike.

"Here you are again, where you don't belong."

"I was just, er, stopping to check my brakes," I said, now worried about the deal I had struck with Lindy to pick up part-time work at the radio station he owned.

He scowled. "And why were you at the garden

dedication for Moriah, anyway? Asking more questions?"

Just then, a delivery man pulled up with a package for the station and had Henry sign for it. I pedaled away, acting like I was leaving, but I only circled the block. As soon as he had left, I hid my bike as best I could in the bushes and ducked inside to find Lindy.

"There you are," she said, walking out from behind her desk where her miniature schnauzers slept.

She gestured toward the dogs. One was white. The other was black with a white mustache. "This is Rachel and Ross. Hope you like drama. These two. They're in a toxic relationship, but I can't resist them."

"Hey," I said nervously, looking around. "Look, I don't think Henry knows I'm working here part-time. Is that going to be a problem?"

"Sweetie, like I said, he comes and goes. He has the office in the back. But I run this radio station."

I let my head fall back in relief.

I spent the next five hours taking calls, as Lindy did her afternoon show. Mostly, people wanted connectedness and positive vibes. Not much was said about prayer, just wanting support as they cared for a sick aunt. Someone had an ongoing dispute with a neighbor over a shared driveway. I even spoke at length to an elderly man who simply said to "pray for surf."

After helping her close, I realized I was at the edge of town and close to the lightkeeper's house. I felt myself being pulled in that direction, and soon, I was pedaling my bicycle into the roadway that led to the house.

I found Gram at the gate, where she had leaned her weathered beach cruiser. She had removed the "No Trespassing" sign and was using scissors to cut it up in an act of defiance. She saw me and threw the pieces of the sign up in the air like confetti.

"Should we be doing that?" I asked nervously, stopping on each word.

Gram threw her hands up. "Let them charge me with trespassing!" She was glowing in the late afternoon sun. She had changed into a white tunic paired with her black pants and black ballet slippers. Her silvery ringlets floated in the wind.

Gram said she had spent part of the afternoon going through the lightkeeper's house to see what work might need to be done before she moved back in. She was on her way out.

I was glad to find her. I needed to go check on a few more things for tomorrow's event. "Want to go with me to meet with the workers who are setting up the drink stations and bonfire in the forest district?"

"You know I love a good bike ride, especially close to sunset," said Gram, kissing me on the cheek.

After I pulled my hair into a ponytail, we set off, pedaling toward the sinking sun. We arrived back at the bakery just as the sun moved behind a purple cloud. We parked our bikes at the back and headed down the forest district trail on foot.

Earlier today, we had seen several crews moving supplies into the forest. One group had been hired to place luminarias along the trail. I had also hired workers to set up drink and food tables and chairs at various stations throughout the trail. Another group had set up our games—a bourbon toss and another called chuck a rubber duck.

Most of the workers had already come and gone, leaving tables and chairs and games covered.

We arrived at the end of the trail facing Lost River Cave to find the firewood crew finishing setting up for our bonfire. We spoke to them before they left, then Gram and I walked closer to the cave. I could feel cold air coming from the entrance. It smelled musty, earthy, and damp.

Gram's gaze grew unfocused. "This cave has been another big part of our family's history."

I sighed, sensing another one of Gram's stories coming on.

I remembered my mom telling me that it had been a bootleg hideaway in the 1920s, then in later years a nightclub.

It was my grandfather, Jessamine Craig, who made alcohol in the cave during the Prohibition. He was about to be brought down by local law enforcement, but Gram, known in the community as Icy Faye Echols (she did not change her name when she married), somehow charmed the sheriff's deputies. She saved the family from losing everything, including the bakery. After Prohibition, she opened a nightclub. In the cave, the cool air was a draw in a time before air conditioning, but after the 1960s, business dropped off, and the club closed.

Today, the cave is still popular with some maritime historians who believed that in the 1700s, a lesser-known pirate, Wainwright "Bird Eye" Skulley, used the cave and surrounding marshes to hide out.

To have Gram tell it, her great-grandfather, Vardy Echols, was thought to have lured Bird Eye and his crew from the cave to the house on Nutwood Street.

Gram, as if sensing my thoughts, began weaving a story.

"My grandfather served them rum laced with

mercury and a compound of drugs and other metals," she said. "The next morning, Bird Eye, his first mate, gunners, boatswains—the lot of them—had been reduced to white squirrels scurrying for nuts in the backyard."

I hated that story when I was a girl because it scared me.

Gram and I stood a little bit longer, not saying anything. I looked up at the longleaf pine trees towering above us. It was beginning to get dark.

I glanced back down to see her walking away.

A rush of cool air escaped the mouth of the cave, making the hair on the back of my neck stand up.

****

Later that evening, I boxed two dozen varieties of pretzel bites, then began preparing my discussion for The Back Porch. I thought about canceling the meeting because I felt defeated and hollowed out on the inside. Living in a small town was supposed to be light and airy. Somehow, I managed to turn my Hallmark movie life into a shaky B movie with bad subplots that made me want to flee and be alone. But with all that was going on, I decided that the writers and their quirks might make for a good distraction. I didn't make too much of a fuss with my clothes, knowing that whatever I chose from Mom's closet would put me in a good mood. I changed into her fuchsia sundress and slipped into the first chunky cardigan that I could find—crimson red.

Again, with all that was going on, I chose the van over my bike. Bread Loaf wouldn't be able to get away quietly should I find myself in danger, but she could tear down the road, if not bang, pop, and splutter.

I turned the key, and soon, I was pulling into one of

the college's many parking lots.

I walked into the faculty house where The Back Porch met just as some in the group were taking their seats. Nissy helped me lay out the pretzel bites on a table with the coffee.

Most of the group talked quietly among themselves. I noticed that Roy Bryce, the weekly newspaper editor and his wife, were talking to the librarian, who seemed to be taking down notes. I was surprised to see Blake and Meg Kidwell at the meeting. They leaned in close to Sam, talking and nodding.

I sensed everyone was picking up where we left off—listing suspects in Moriah's death. But before they could derail us, I wanted to at least try to stick with our schedule.

We hadn't finished discussing conflict last time, and I pulled out my notes.

I walked to the front to get their attention. "Who can tell us the difference between internal conflict and external conflict?"

Roy was the first with his hand up. "Internal is something the character struggles with deep down inside. External, that's when they're up against someone or something."

"That's right, and usually, in detective fiction, a suspect may show one conflict but hide another," I said.

Meg raised her hand to add to that. "Or you might know that they are in conflict with another person but not know exactly what that conflict is. You have to look at what's not there. What they're not saying."

"Like with Henry Cherry." Nissy sat up straighter. "We know he had to go to Moriah to be bailed out financially, but that wasn't his only financial resource or only way out. He needed her for some other reason."

I sighed. This was not where I wanted our discussion to go, but maybe she had a point. What was I missing? Was it possible that Henry also wanted to sell those Beet Boxes? But why? He already had lots of businesses. Yes, some had not done so well and were failing, but what was it about those Beet Boxes that made half this town want to kill for them?

Sam, who had been sitting quietly in the back, cleared his throat. "And what about Carlisle? What was it that came between them?"

We were missing something. *But what?*

We were near the end of our meeting, so Corrine took it upon herself to walk to the dry-erase board and begin listing our suspects.

I let out a heavy sigh and walked to the front because I couldn't bear it any longer.

Much to Corrine's chagrin, I erased her list.

I wrote two words on the board: *Beet Box.* I drew a rectangle around the words, then arrows shooting away from that listing people connected to Moriah's business, or people who wanted to play a part in her business.

The first arrow pointed to Henry Cherry. He had gone to see Moriah at her office. He had a lot to lose when they divorced. He needed money from her.

Then, I wrote down Carlisle's name. She was in some sort of dispute with Moriah about the Beet Boxes they had been selling at the farmer's market.

Next, I drew an arrow and wrote down the student's name, Jessie. As an adjunct professor myself, I knew that students complain sometimes. There was always going to be a request from time to time for a change of grade, but could a student be desperate enough that they would kill over that?

Then, as much as I hated to write the next name, I put it up there for all to see: *Cal*.

His idea to start a competing business and sell pre-made meals at the farmer's market had been met with opposition. Why had Moriah gone to so much trouble to shut him out? Would Cal kill someone over that?

Chapter 14

Early the next morning, I left Mouse in bed and pulled on my softest yoga pants. I went to my mom's closet and reached for a box in the back that contained an old quilt top she had never finished. I unfolded it and inhaled. It smelled, well, like Mom. Sunshine and cotton. I wrapped myself in her favorite colors—orchid, lilac, and lavender. Some of the quilt blocks had been cut from soft, nearly threadbare denim.

I walked quietly down the spiral staircase. Downstairs, the bakery was dark, and though the sun wasn't up, I could see through the windows that it was just beginning to get light on the horizon.

I made coffee and grabbed an Irish cross pretzel from a container in the back. I walked outside to see several stars still visible, as well as the moon. There was no wind, only calm. The ocean seemed more like a lake this morning. I could hear a gentle lapping, as the tide had already moved out. The air smelled briny but fresh, like it does after a heavy rain. *Ten years ago today,* I thought. *Brie, wherever you are, I miss you. Today is for you.*

I sat at one of the cafe tables, wrapped in the quilt top, and waited. Soon enough, Hazel made her appearance. I offered her a piece of the pretzel. "Hey, lady."

She looked at me inquisitively. She was patient.

"This is a big day. Do you think I'm ready?" I asked.

After a few minutes, I walked away from Hazel but turned back to see her eating the pretzel. She seemed to answer me by pointing her head to the end of our deck, which led to the forest district trailhead.

I breathed in a simple prayer for healing and finding lost souls, then walked back inside to shower. Standing in my robe, I decided to wear Mom's cut-off blue jean shorts and an off-the-shoulder ruffly blouse the color of mint.

I paired both with the Birkenstock sandals, then took a selfie in front of the mirror. I was feeling anticipation for the night's event and a little giddy at the fact that I was going to try to increase interest once again in Brie's case. I had kicked out my right toe in the picture, emphasizing the well-worn sandals, feeling like I was in middle school again with Brie.

Me:—*If you were in Seabrook right now, we could take these vintage cuties to get Mermaid teas. Come home, B.*—

I waited a few seconds. But I knew. The police had always told us that it was likely she wasn't still alive. Whatever had happened to her that night ten years ago, it was the first twenty-four hours that were the most important. As the days and weeks went on, the chances of finding her alive became slim to none. The search, after a few months, focused on the recovery of a body.

Brie, even on the off chance that she was still out there, would have switched phones by now or phone numbers. I knew. But I like the idea of keeping her alive in my heart.

****

In the bakery, I tried to keep my mind off Brie. I hadn't really considered the full weight of the tenth anniversary of her disappearance. How it wasn't really an occasion to be marked, but more like a grim reminder of how much we had lost that night all those years ago.

To shake it off, I decided to do what I usually did. I just got to work, going through a list of items that needed to be completed before half of Seabrook started to arrive later that afternoon for Cocktails and Trails.

I wanted townspeople who had been reluctant to come back to the White Squirrel to experience a drink and food menu crafted with love. I planned to start with a cocktail hour on the deck under festival lights. Workers had already brought over six high-top tables, borrowed from Nissy. I had purchased eight more, using money from teaching the night class. The high-top tables would encourage people to stand around, mixing and mingling.

I had planned two signature cocktails. A Blackberry Smash comprising blackberry whiskey, club soda, and lime juice served in Mason jars. And my personal twist on a throwback, a Pink Squirrel—white chocolate liqueur and vanilla ice cream. I used a tiny cookie scoop for the ice cream, and I included a splash of almond crème liqueur, which was red, giving the drink a pastel pink color under freshly grated nutmeg. It was an adult milkshake in a martini glass. I meant it to be an ode to my mother, who bought us each one at a hotel bar in Savannah after helping me move into the dorm and declaring that I "was a woman now, capable of making my own decisions and living with my own mistakes." Before we had toasted my newfound adulthood, she had said, "Or you could just be yourself" and pulled me in for a hug.

I closed my eyes, missing her right now as we dressed up the bakery. She loved this kind of thing. I looked out to see Gram and Cal stocking the first drink station on the deck. In case cocktails weren't someone's thing, I had included one mocktail, an Orange-Mango Crush that required loading a blender full of orange juice, mango sorbet, milk, and a splash of grenadine before pouring into sugar-rimmed wine glasses.

I also made sure soda and water were available at all three drink stations. In addition to the deck, we included one drink station at the edge of the forest district where the coastal pines opened to the state park that hugged our coastline north of town. There would be propane fire tables at each drink and food station, games, as well as a table showcasing the needs of the college and a chance to make a monetary donation. I wanted everyone attending to enjoy an amazing night. The best part, with the trail illuminated, people could get out among the coastal pines at night.

The last stop of the evening would be at the end of the trail, which led to steps to the Lost River Cave.

Workers had already set up a small stage and podium for speeches in front of the bonfire.

Everything was coming together.

By mid-morning, I was helping Gram and Cal as they prepped the pretzel slider trays: meatball po'boy, croque monsieur, and citrus chicken with jalapeno cream cheese dip.

For dessert, I had outsourced: Nissy's pie shooters. Everyone loved her pies in shot glasses. I chose three flavors: strawberry cheesecake, apple caramel, and, of course, lemon meringue.

Nissy delivered them herself. She wouldn't let me

pay her, though! I made a mental note to secretly repay her another way. I knew she had a birthday coming up.

Later in the day, with Gram and Cal helping to string festival lights on the deck, I was free to pick up the produce.

I found Mouse still in bed and blew raspberries on his belly and around his neck. "Who's ready for the farmer's market?"

He answered by running in circles on my bed and darting away each time I tried to scoop him up. He barked and wagged his tail. We loaded into Bread Loaf, windows down, beagle ears flapping.

At the market, I bought vegetables and fruit for our grazing boards. I had also planned trays of vegetarian charcuterie kabobs with cheese, veggies, and fruit.

Mouse and I also made a stop at Forgotten Coast Coffee for a latte and a pup cup.

My last stop was at Ana's table. In addition to jewelry, she sold prayer candles. I wanted to have a candle for Brie at the event. I had been reading Mom's book, but I still wasn't sure if I would utter another word from it. I just knew that Brie might need something bright to light the way home. I was toying with the idea of creating a small shrine at one of the drink stations next to a sign letting townspeople know about Brie's unsolved case.

"This one," said Ana, bringing out a tall white candle in a glass holder. "It'll bring her home. It's the luz de gracia. Light of grace."

Ana was beautiful, as always. And being around her made me feel beautiful, too, because she just had a way with people and an ability to make you feel loved. She was wearing a cornflower blue tunic and white yoga pants with sandals. A beaded necklace with disks representing the twelve chakras hung low on her neck. Her cropped hair was black, parted to the side, and I could see gold hoops hanging from her ears.

She examined me for a second, then asked about the dusty blue choker. "How are you enjoying it?"

"Well, I lost the pendant. I feel horrible."

She reached out to touch my arm, then brought me in for a hug. "I know you have been going through a lot lately," she said.

"That's putting it mildly," I said, laughing a little.

"Don't worry. It'll turn up," said Ana, whose confidence seemed to be tapped from an endless well of resolve and gratitude. "If you've lost something and you love it, it'll come back to you."

Chapter 15

The evening was spectacular, one of those rare times when you're reminded how special your own little place in the world really is. Dress was black tie optional, and for Seabrook men, that meant laid-back, easy-going button-down shirts, with colorful bow ties, navy blazers, and khakis. For the ladies, most chose simple shift dresses with gauzy pastel shawls. A few women who had just come from their offices straight to the event traded heels for flats and sandals before walking up. Artists in town wore tunics and wide, dressy pants. Gram, of course, stole the show in her leopard print duster, black pants, and layers of gold and silver beads around her neck.

The bakery glowed from a distance. The sun was setting, casting an orange glow on everything. Townspeople stood under the festival lights enjoying drinks and pretzel sliders on the deck, which overlooked the sugar-white sand and turquoise water.

On one side of the White Squirrel, the ocean waves ebbed and flowed, creating a relaxing rhythm. On the other, the coastal pine forest created a backdrop of dark blue and green. From the deck, townspeople could also see the hiking trail illuminated and smell the bonfire in the distance.

I handed out maps of the trail that showed each drink and food stop. I wore Mom's ruffly, breezy gypsy dress.

It had bell sleeves and a V-neck, and I had tied a brown belt around the middle. The color matched my steel blue eyes. I had taken a lot of time with my hair, perfecting the beachy waves I had tried earlier in the week.

Fin arrived with Shea, holding hands. It was the first time I had seen him in a tie. He wore dark blue pants that matched his sports coat. She wore a green sundress with a blue daisy pattern, her golden hair in a side braid on one shoulder.

I ran into Carlisle at the bourbon toss. She was having a hard time throwing a ring onto a hook attached to a board. She was determined to get a shot of bourbon, but every time she missed, if she wanted another chance at getting a drink, she had to fork over five dollars.

She noticed me laughing after she missed the last shot.

"Casey June, this is rigged." She folded her arms tightly across her chest.

"Well, it is a fund-raiser. Think of all the money you're spending going to a good cause." I gently bit my lip.

Finally, she quit. She was turning to leave when she paused and looked back.

"I do have some more information for you, but not here," Carlisle said. "Can you meet me tomorrow for lunch? Twelve thirty?"

"Sure," I said, rocking slightly and finding it difficult to breathe.

"Let me have your number," she said, handing over her phone. She had already opened a screen for new contacts.

I took Carlisle's phone, punched in my number, then she gave her number to me.

I looked around to see Gram coming up the trail. Cal was leaning against a tree and watching me.

At about nine o'clock, most of the revelers had winded their way through the trail and to the bonfire, where embers rose up into the night sky at the entrance of the cave. I noticed Nissy had made her way down. The air was beginning to cool, and you could still hear the gentle lapping of the ocean. The moon had risen above the water and was visible through the trees.

I noticed Sam had finally made it. He was dressed head to toe in black—button-down shirt, pants, and what looked to be a new pair of black cowboy boots.

While townspeople were still busy talking among themselves, I went over to a flat rock and lit the white candle next to a picture of Brie.

I looked at Gram. It was time for me to introduce the college's philanthropy chair. She winked.

I started my speech with a simple thank you. "You all know the history of my family's bakery and how important it is to this town. You should also know how important this town was to my mother, who passed away a few months ago near these caves. If you'll join me in a moment of silence, I would be grateful."

Everyone bowed their heads. Then, all we could hear was the breeze in the tree branches and the ocean. Suddenly, a strong wind blew through. I looked up to see an owl fly over.

After taking a deep breath and taking a step back, I continued with my speech. "This is also the tenth anniversary of the disappearance of Brie Kidwell, one of Seabrook's own. It's surreal to me how long it's been. Her disappearance has impacted my life in ways I am still struggling to understand."

I looked at Brie's parents, Blake and Meg Kidwell. They held each other tight.

Then, I walked up to the bonfire and tossed a letter Brie had written to me when I found out she loved Cal. I had never told anyone. *It was time to let it go and forgive her.* "Miss you every day, Brie," I said, pausing, then rushing to add, "Now, please join me in welcoming Mills Banks, Seabrook Community College's director of philanthropy."

Mills, whose pale skin contrasted with his thick black hair, shot me a look, then pursed his lips. He made his way to the small riser and delivered a speech about the importance of a college town supporting its students. Afterward, he shook a few hands and spoke to major donors, folks looking to put their names on classroom buildings.

The event winded down at about one o'clock in the morning. People took their time leaving. Blake and Meg Kidwell thanked me and brought me in for a squeeze. Fin left carrying Shea, who had fallen asleep in a quilt at the bonfire.

Gram and I were busy doing clean up until the wee morning hours. Sam stayed to help.

Hours later, Sam and I decided to make coffee in the bakery. We were still sitting at a table eating leftover pie shooters when Gram called it a night and went upstairs with Mouse and Lean Cuisine.

Sam reached into this pocket. "The police have finished looking at Moriah's office on campus," he said, holding up a key. "I decided I can't be found snooping around through professors' offices but..." He paused as he laid the key on the table.

I smiled. "But if you laid this down or forgot this

and someone picked it up ..."

He smiled back and turned to leave.

****

I had barely laid my head down to sleep when my alarm went off at five o'clock. I was tired but still riding high from the previous night's success. I took a quick shower and stood in a bathrobe in front of Mom's closet, looking for something. She had the most worn and lived-in blue jean overalls that I can ever remember someone wearing. I had loved those on her, but as a teenager, I had been secretly embarrassed because none of the other mothers wore things like that. They wore blouses and skirts that went straight to the knee with pantyhose and heels. At the beach, they wore one-piece swimsuits and modest cover-ups. Not my mom. She wore string bikinis and crocheted shawls.

I kept digging in the closet until I found a stack of clothing folded neatly on a shelf. *Bingo*. I unfolded the overalls. Then, I brushed the softest denim I have ever known against my cheek.

It was the first real warm day of spring, and I paired them with a white V-neck T-shirt. I put the key that Sam had given me in my hip pocket, scrubbed Mouse's little velvet head, and headed downstairs to the bakery.

Gram waved at me from behind the counter as I slipped out with a thin mint pretzel bite.

Soon, I was pedaling my bike through the gate of the college and then a parking lot.

I had a spring in my step as I got off my bike. It was a beautiful day on campus. I walked through a courtyard where forsythia and azalea were in bloom. Nearby, students had gathered on park benches and at picnic tables. They were eating lunch and reading. Two students were playing with a hacky sack. Another was relaxing in a hammock.

I looked down to see Lean Cuisine had found me.

She nuzzled against my legs every third or fourth step, so I decided to push my bike across campus, rather than speeding away and ditching her. Though Lean Cuisine usually had my back and warned me when something was getting ready to happen, I had an unusual feeling that I needed to be the one watching out for her.

I stopped at the courtyard on the east end of campus we called The Grove and leaned my bike against a picnic table. I reached for my bag and pulled out a pretzel bite for Lean Cuisine. I sat with my legs folded on a park bench and smoothed the faded overalls, which felt like butter against my skin.

I looked up to see two students walking over.

"Hey, Ms. Hart." Belmara was a petite twenty-something who wore no make-up on her flawless brown skin and simply parted her bobbed black hair down the middle.

"Belmara, good to see you," I said, remembering that she sat in the front row of my class.

"This your cat?" she asked.

"In some ways, she's more than a cat to me," I said, beaming back up at them.

I realized I had been in such a rush all semester to make sure that students documented sources and that their verbs and nouns agreed that I hadn't really taken the time to just talk to them. *They were people. They liked cats.*

Belmara wore a T-shirt and running shorts and bent to stroke Lean Cuisine's back.

I didn't recognize the other student, a pale young

woman who had to be close to Belmara's age. She had on similar clothes and wore her sandy hair in French braids down each side. "I'm Jessie," she said.

I sat up. "You didn't happen to have Ms. Moore last semester for Ethics, did you?"

"I did. It was one of the hardest classes that I have taken so far. She acted like we were in law school. One of our assignments was to review and edit a business plan for her. I had an 88.9 percent at the end, and she wouldn't bring it up to an A."

"Did you file a complaint?"

"I did. I was trying to get into nursing, which requires a high GPA, but I didn't get anywhere with it. The syllabus states that she doesn't round up final grades, so I let it go," said Jessie, whose face dropped. "I heard she died."

Jessie looked down for a beat, then remembered something. "You know, one strange thing that happened last semester—her law partner contacted some of us from class. She wanted to see the business plan that we had been working on for Ms. Moore. But nobody offered it up. We only worked on hard copies in class and had to return them when class ended."

"I'm sorry that she put you and the other students in that position," I said.

"It doesn't matter now," said Jessie, "I'm not trying to get into nursing anymore. I think I want to be a writer, like Belmara."

More students began to cross campus, and it was almost time for the next class to begin. They started to turn to leave, and I stood up. "Wait, I have something for you."

I reached into my bag and dug out two new journals

and two of my favorite pens—in purple. "If you want to be a writer, you should start keeping a journal. Write everything down."

"Thanks," said Jessie.

"You know, Ms. H," said Belmara, who turned back to face me. "You look cute today. Those are some sweet overalls."

Chapter 16

With that new information, the key to Moriah's office was burning a hole in my pocket.

After the students left, I gathered my things and walked across campus to the building that houses adjunct faculty offices. Once inside, I found her office door, removed the police tape, and stood there for a beat to make sure no one was nearby. *This was not the day to run into the dean.*

When all was clear, I unlocked the door and closed it behind me. Moriah's office looked like most adjunct professors' offices—not much in the way of decoration or awards or degrees. That would all be in her law office. Here, she just kept a few essentials. She likely used this office to prep for class and store student records.

I pulled out her chair and sat down. I did a quick scan of her desk. She had a computer monitor and keyboard. There was a mug filled with pens and pencils. I found a stash of candy in one drawer and a stack of trade magazines in the other.

In the corner, there was a faux Ficus tree. Her bulletin board only had a calendar. Looking around, the place was lacking any personal touches.

I sat there for a few seconds thinking, ready to give up. Then, I looked again at the door. There was a canvas Seabrook Farmer's Market bag hanging on a hook. She probably had tons of those. It didn't look like it held anything, but I reached for it anyway.

Inside, I found a takeout menu and a flyer for the farmer's market, but there was a thin manilla folder, too. I pulled out the folder and opened it, turning each page slowly. There was a business plan for Beet Box that originally included Moriah and Carlisle as equal partners. Behind it, an updated business plan included a loan for Beet Box, though only showed Moriah as the owner. There was also a file showing Henry had proposed a development near the lightkeeper's quarters, my family's home, along the disputed roadway. Beet Box eventually would move to the development and be an anchor business to a strip mall that would include a smoothie bar and an Auntie Anne's—a national pretzel chain store!

I pulled my phone from my hip pocket and snapped a photo of each page.

As I finished, I heard a voice outside the door. I recognized the voice of a janitor, and he was talking to someone who spoke in hushed tones. The janitor seemed to be answering questions. I panicked, folded the papers and stuffed them in my hip pocket.

As I pivoted on one foot, I saw the doorknob turning. Then, I heard a familiar voice.

"What's going on in here?" Fin pushed open the door. I slowly faced him.

"Nothing." *Just a little breaking and entering.* My heart was racing.

Fin dipped his chin and raised his eyebrows, waiting.

"Moriah was a member of the writing club. I got a key to pick up any club materials stored in her office."

"You expect me to believe that?"

"Seems perfectly reasonable to me. She was at one of our meetings the week before she passed away."

"Murdered is more like it. Casey June, you know you're still a suspect." His voice rose in intensity.

"When you put it like that, you make me feel guilty for being in here."

"As you should. You completely ignored the police tape. Let me do my job and handle this investigation." A hard expression cemented his face.

"While police are busy focusing on me, the real killer is out there," I muttered tearfully to myself. "In the meantime, people are afraid to eat at the White Squirrel."

Fin looked down and shook his head.

I slowly moved the Beet Box papers from my pocket and handed them to him. "You need to see this."

He reached for the papers reluctantly. "We've already searched this office. I can't imagine that you turned up something we haven't already found, processed, and returned."

But as soon as he began to read the papers, it dawned on him.

He looked up, jaw clenching. "Moriah cut Carlisle out of the business."

****

Fin offered to drive me back to the bakery, but I turned him down. We left campus without him scolding me and without me questioning his investigation. There was still tension between us, but we seemed to reach some sort of understanding. Of course, he reminded me to be careful as he walked me to my bike. Then, he did something unexpected. He side-hugged me, the way we used to in high school, and said, "I'm glad you're back in town."

I was speechless and only offered "me, too" as I put my arm around his firm shoulders and returned the hug. He was cool to the touch and left me feeling like I had just gone under a wave and was having trouble resurfacing.

****

Back at the bakery apartment, I found Lean Cuisine waiting for me. Gram had let her inside. I headed for the living room. The cat followed, with Mouse trailing behind.

I made a nest with throw pillows and blankets and sunk into the couch. With my animal family happily sandwiching me on either side, I opened my laptop so that I could find out more about the Beet Box business. After a few searches and scrolling through social media, I found a review from a man whom Carlisle charged for a week's worth of meals, but when he picked them up, she had shorted him three. Another review also specifically named Carlisle. She completely forgot to make a week's worth of meals for a big client.

I closed my laptop. I needed to make a trip to Lucky Beach to ask Moriah's sister a few more questions.

I left Mouse and Lean Cuisine cuddled together on the couch and tiptoed downstairs. Outside, the sun was low in the sky. I walked down Nutwood Street and turned onto Main Street to see suntanned couples holding hands and heading into restaurants. I saw Shea pulling a red wagon loaded with beach chairs and a cooler. She waved from across the street. I waved back, noticing Marilu following close behind, giving me, as they say in the South, "a look."

In a few minutes, I was at Lucky Beach, which was beginning to fill with people coming off the beach. A line had formed at the register. I saw Moriah's sister, Jenna, wiping down tables. I waved. She recognized me, hesitated, and then walked over.

"Casey June," she said. "Need your Mermaid tea?"

"I might try something different tonight, but I wanted to ask you something first about Moriah and Carlisle when they started Beet Box. I saw online that people were complaining about Carlisle."

"Oh, yeah, people were furious, so Moriah ditched her," she said.

"Wouldn't Moriah have had to buy her out?"

"They hadn't officially incorporated the business. They hadn't invested any of their money in it. So, Moriah saw that as her out. She dropped Carlisle, then turned right around and put a copyright on Beet Box and filed as a corporation."

****

I left Lucky Beach with a loaded tea called Sunset— pink, orange and a pomegranate red.

The sun was getting close to dipping into the horizon.

I was absorbed in what Jenna had said. I decided to keep walking past the bakery. I wanted to be alone with my thoughts. I knew that Carlisle now had motive and means. She also had left the bakery the day Moriah died with the pint of jalapeno pimento cheese. But could I place her at the gate that night? Did anyone see her?

I was also still working through my issues with Gram. We had made up, but I didn't know if I was ready to jump broomstick and cauldron into her insistence that not only did she turn my mom into a cat, but that mom had cast spells of her own, even publishing a book about it.

Suddenly, I realized I was walking toward Lost River Cave.

There are two ways to get there. Through the maritime forest or along the beach, which starts as sugar white sand but before you get to the main cave the terrain becomes rocky, featuring dramatic cliffs that lead to smaller sea caves. The Lost River is actually a tidal river and flows into the main cave entrance from the sea.

I walked in that direction along the beach. I felt the softness of the overalls, the last of the day's sun on my skin. Finally, as I reached the rocks, I looked out onto the ocean where mom had gone under. That's when I knew I wouldn't be returning to Atlanta. I was no longer business suits, strappy heels, and nine dollar avocado toasts.

I looked down at the overalls that hugged my body and smiled. I was sun-bleached denim, sandals, and gooey turtle pretzels.

I had to be myself.

****

By the time I returned home, it was getting dark, and the wind was picking up. I could hear the waves crashing along the beach and see seaweed collecting each time the water went back out. The tide was coming in.

Gram was in the bakery, rinsing one of the coffeepots and wiping it clean. She brought a shaky hand to her forehead.

"I've got it from here," I said, reaching for some tongs that needed to be put in the dishwasher.

"Sure?" she asked.

I squeezed her hand and kissed her cheek. "Go on. I'll be up in a while."

After she left, I started turning off some of the lights.

I found Mouse finishing a thorough sweep of the bakery dining area, looking for crumbs, when my phone vibrated in my pocket.

It was Sam:

—*Are you home?*—

Me:—*Yes, and I found something today. Can you come over?*—

Sam:—*Walking over now.*—

I was still looking down at my phone as I unlocked the door. It swung open wildly, and Mouse ran out into the wind. I walked out in bare feet. He usually didn't go too far unless he saw a squirrel or got spooked. Then, a flash of lightning crossed the night sky. A few seconds later, there was a clap of thunder. Mouse took off and growled at something. I was running down the front steps after him when something hard came crashing down on my head.

I lay there on the sidewalk. I heard a car in the distance, tires squealing, then a dog's yelp.

Chapter 17

I heard my name and felt a cool cloth on my forehead.

"Casey June."

"Yes," I managed weakly. I realized I was lying on the ground.

I saw Fin hovering over me and the flash of lights in the background. First responders lifted me onto a gurney, and I was being wheeled toward an ambulance.

I suddenly remembered Mouse getting loose and the sound of the car. I reached out for Fin's hand and shivered. "Where's Mouse?"

"He's going to be okay," said Fin in a guarded tone. He looked down for a beat, took off his jacket, and put it over me. "He's pretty beat up. He's with Cal at the turtle hospital."

My head felt like it was being squeezed in a vise. A stream of tears fell down my face. I squeezed Fin's hand. "I want to go see him."

"We need to get you checked out first. Then, I promise I'll take you to him," said Fin, pausing and taking a very long time to inhale and exhale. "What do you remember?"

"I got a text from Sam. He said he would be right over. I unlocked the door, and it was like someone pulled it open violently. Mouse got loose, and that's when someone hit me. Sam wasn't here when you arrived?"

"No," he said. "I didn't see any lights on next door either. We think Mouse bit your assailant, though, before he was hit by the car. Your grandmother heard the commotion and found you both. There was blood, a pretty significant amount, near where you were found. You have some lacerations, but we've ruled out that the other blood could be yours."

The EMT interrupted us and said he needed to get me to the hospital.

I released Fin's hand, and he drew in close to my face, brushing my hair back from my eye. "Please stop investigating on your own."

****

At the hospital, I learned I had a concussion. The doctor told me I could go home that night, but I was under strict orders to rest for the next twenty-four hours.

Gram walked into my examination room just as I was putting on Fin's jacket. She came over and pulled me into her. I cried and snorted and whimpered about Mouse.

She just said over and over again, "I know. I know."

I told her I was sorry about how I acted growing up, embarrassed by our family, not coming home when Mom died, not believing Gram about the cat. Finally, I raised up from her shoulder and said simply, "I love you."

"I love you to the moon and back, June Bug," she said.

She motioned for me to sit down on the hospital bed, and she pulled up one of the chairs in the room as close to the bed as she could get it. Then, she plopped down, tired with worry and relief washing over her face.

"Oh," said Gram, remembering something. She

reached into her purse. "Here," she said, handing my phone to me.

She had found it on the sidewalk outside of the bakery. There were several new messages from Sam. One saying that he had been pulled away due to a matter on campus. Another said he had heard what happened. He wanted to know if I was okay.

I texted him:

—*I'm scared, but I'm okay. Worried. Mouse is pretty beat up.*—

Gram had also brought a brown paper shopping bag and pulled out a pastry box, as well as an old photo album. We spent the next hour eating chocolate peanut butter lava pretzel bombs and looking at old pictures. The photo album was one that I had never seen before. There were pictures of my mom before she met my dad and pictures after they married.

"Have I ever told you the story of how your mom and dad met?" she asked.

I shook my head, and because I was still very emotional, I let more tears fall again.

"Well, he was a neighbor's boy, and he started coming over to play when they were about ten. He would bring all manner of seashells and rocks, and they would play for hours along the shore, down by the caves. I never knew where I would find them when it came time for dinner."

"So they started as friends?"

"Mmm, hmmm," said Gram, looking wistful.

"What was dad like as a boy?" I lightly clasped my hands around hers.

"Well, he had hair the color of driftwood. His eyes were like diamonds. Not really blue, so much as a ray of light. The color shimmered and danced." She stroked my palm. "You know how some people look like their personalities? Well, he was like that. Being around him, everything sparkled."

She continued. "When he died so young, after they had just had you, it took the shine out of everything for a while."

In one picture, Mom wore the baggy overalls I had on. She looked to be barely pregnant with me. I started crying again when I glanced down and found blood from the lacerations on my face had stained the front of them.

"Don't worry, honey. I can get that out," said Gram, coming in for another hug.

We passed an hour like that. Crying. Hugging. Eating. Marveling at the photos of my mom. My pain killers were kicking in, and as always, Gram's food was good medicine.

A while later, a nurse came in and said we were free to leave.

As we were packing up Gram's picnic, we heard the sound of cowboy boot heels.

Sam came in with a drink carrier that held four cups. He wore a green checked shirt that made his hazel eyes seem warmer, nearly green. Of course, he had on his tight black jeans.

"For you," he said, handing a coffee to me.

He had guessed that Gram would want tea and had brought two different kinds—mint and blueberry hibiscus.

She took both. "It's been a long night."

I took one sip of my coffee and realized it was the German chocolate-flavored coffee with coconut creamer and salted caramel syrup. *He remembered.*

I looked to see the Beachy Bean logo on the side of the cup. *What had he been doing on Jekyll Island after going to campus tonight?*

Before I could ask him, though, he shifted uncomfortably. He said he knew there wasn't a lot he could do for me right now, but if my favorite cup of coffee could help, then it was worth the drive.

"Besides, I had a craving for Turtle Love," he said, holding the other cup of coffee, raising his eyebrows and widening his now-watery eyes in a vulnerable way that I had not seen before.

"I have something for you, too," I said, handing him the key to Moriah's office. "Thanks."

As we walked out of the hospital together, I filled him in on how Moriah had cut Carlisle out of the Beet Box business. I also told him what I learned from Jenna, that Carlisle had made customers angry by not filling orders.

****

Gram said she would take me to the vet clinic inside the turtle hospital to see Mouse. Sam followed us to make sure we made it safely, then waved as we walked through the front doors.

"Brace yourself," Gram said. "Mouse doesn't look the way you remember him."

I sucked in a ragged breath, and after asking a receptionist, we were led through double doors and met a vet technician in the back. A light was on in an exam room, and the tech indicated with a nod that we could enter. I opened the door slowly to find my dog sedated on a small cot on the floor. His eyes were swollen shut, and he had lacerations on his nose and midsection. One ear had stitches where it had been torn. One of his hind legs was wrapped in gauze.

Cal sat cross-legged on the floor, stroking Mouse's forehead.

"Hey," I said in a hushed tone.

Cal turned to look at us and motioned us over. He only worked part-time as an assistant. Though he had finished veterinarian school and was a doctor, he had graduated when the job market was tight, and he didn't want to open his own practice. Since Seabrook didn't have a stand-alone veterinarian clinic, most people in our town took their pets to the turtle hospital, which employed two veterinarians and a host of vet technicians.

As Gram and I bent down over Mouse, Cal rose and rubbed the small of my back. He leaned in to say, "I'll get some floor pillows and blankets. It's going to be a long night."

As Gram held me, I bawled and choked and wailed as I took everything in. Finally, I sat down next to Mouse and stroked his nose.

After Cal came back, Gram got me settled with the blankets and pillows on the floor. She reached down to hug me and Cal, then left us to talk.

"Will he be all right?" I asked.

Cal adjusted his horn-rimmed glasses and relayed information given to him earlier from the veterinarian treating Mouse. He spoke gently. "I'm afraid he was hit head-on. There's a lot of bruising. He had a collapsed lung. If he makes it through the night, he will need surgery to repair a fracture to his leg."

I nodded.

Cal continued. "It's a pretty sophisticated surgery, and this kind of repair requires titanium pins in his leg to reset the bone. He will have to wear an exoskeleton for at least three months.

"The surgery will cost twenty-two hundred dollars. This doesn't include his rehabilitation and follow-up visits."

I looked down at Mouse, who seemed to realize I was there. He let out a pitifully small moan.

I moved my hand to Mouse's forehead.

Cal placed his hand on mine. "Casey June, if Mouse doesn't have this surgery, he will have to be put down."

Chapter 18

I woke up at the vet's office with a knot on my head.

Mouse slept wearily next to me. He was no longer sedated.

The swelling made it impossible for him to open his eyes and see me, but he knew I was there. If I moved my hand away from his forehead, he whimpered.

Overnight, Gram had returned with breakfast. There was a pastry box on the chair next to my bag. I opened it to find a pretzel sandwich with bacon, egg, and cheese.

Gram had brought me a change of clothes. She had also left her vintage thermos, the kind with a plastic mug on top. It had a card tied to it, labeling the contents: Cadillac Coffee. I opened the note to find her messy handwriting: *You remember all those slider pretzel buns that Cal and I had to make? Well, this is how we did it: hot chocolate mix, creamer, and coffee granules. Drink up; it's going to be a long day. Hang in there, honey. Love, Gram.*

Using one hand, I opened the thermos and poured the coffee into the plastic cup. I took a slow sip and sighed. How was I going to pay for Mouse's surgery? How was I going to fight the lawsuit? Clear my name? The bakery's reputation? Would the attacker return? Could Gram be in danger?

I texted Brie:

—*How am I going to do all of this?*—

I sat my phone down on the windowsill above where Mouse lay. Sunlight was beginning to pour in.

I was rubbing my eyes when I noticed that behind the thermos, she had included a small plastic container. There was a piece of masking tape across it, and Gram had written Mouse's name and below it the words "Give this to him when he wakes." I opened it to find whipped cream with crumbled bacon and a drizzle of what smelled like pancake syrup.

I raised my eyebrows and looked at Mouse. "You got a pup cup."

He lifted his nose, smelling the bacon. I wasn't sure I was supposed to give him anything, but I didn't know how much longer I had with him. If anything, right now, brought him even a little comfort, I was willing to do it.

Mouse lifted his mouth just enough to lick the contents from the plastic container and let out a feeble moan of appreciation.

About an hour later, Cal walked through to check on Mouse. He used a light to look into Mouse's eyes. Then, he examined Mouse's wounds. I took one look at Cal and loved the man who had broken my heart all over again— messy hair, torn T-shirt, cargo shorts, and all. He was so tender with Mouse, in fact, all animals.

Cal turned to me and asked if I wanted a ride home.

I couldn't even mumble the words. I nodded, collected my things, and kissed Mouse gently above his eyes.

I followed Cal outside to find him heading toward his white 1980 Volkswagen Rabbit. "I forgot about this," I said, offering a weak smile.

"She still gets me down the road," he said. "You, me, and Brie had a lot of good times in high school driving this boneshaker around. What do they say? Everyone should own a convertible at least once in their lifetime. I guess in my case, it's the only car I've ever owned."

I smiled to myself, feeling a little of the gravity of Mouse's condition lift.

Inside Cal's car, we buckled up, and I turned to put my bag in the back when I saw a cooler. "Do you happen to have any water in there?"

"Help yourself."

I reached into the cooler, grabbed water, and saw two containers at the bottom labeled Beet Box. When Moriah died, her booth had closed at the farmer's market.

"Where did you get those Beet Boxes?" I asked, feeling a knot in my stomach.

"Oh, those. I had a few extras in the freezer. Before, you know," said Cal, acting nervous.

****

Cal dropped me off at the bakery, and I walked around the back so I could sneak upstairs without customers seeing me. My hair was a disaster, and I could feel the grime on my skin.

I walked into the apartment to find that Gram had already packed some boxes for her move back to the lightkeeper's house. Seeing those made me sad. I didn't have enough energy left to be angry, though.

Soon, I was taking what seemed to be the longest shower of my life. I put on my pink terry robe and headed to the papasan chair, and opened my laptop. I looked up the value of Volkswagen vans, thinking of selling our beloved Bread Loaf for Mouse's surgery.

A million other things were also running through my

mind. I did a search on Moriah's booth at the farmer's market. Sure enough, no one had been able to buy more Beet Boxes. Several people had posted in a chat that they depended on them for portion control. One person admitted they just didn't like cooking. Whichever camp they were in, people in Seabrook wanted their Beet Boxes. How did Cal get those? Had he been to Moriah's house?

After putting away my laptop, I took a deep breath and looked into the closet. I remembered another piece of clothing that my mother used to wear, an amazing maxi skirt with a split front and ruffle along the hem. It was gunmetal gray, and she would often pair it with a rust orange tank and gauzy, cropped, dark purple wrap sweater. I found all three hanging near the front of the closet like she had just stepped away. I put them on and slipped into Mom's suede Birkenstock sandals.

I was at home in these clothes. They were soft and stretchy, and the fibers and colors made me happy. I let my hair air dry, tucking the ends of my bobbed brown hair behind my ears, then walked downstairs to the bakery.

****

Inside the White Squirrel, every cafe table was filled with people, and there was a line at the register. I noticed Brie's parents behind the counter with Gram. I was guessing since their tasting room was only open Thursday through Saturday that Gram had recruited them for the day. Gram was tying an apron around Meg Kidwell and, at the same time, looking pointedly at Blake Kidwell as she rattled off what needed to be brought out from the sheet pans in the back to the front counter display case. Brie's parents had made an art out of pouring wines and hosting events at Watermelon Creek. Here, they looked like they had swum out too far and gotten caught in a rip current.

Gram motioned for me at the bar. Shea was standing with her.

"Casey June, meet your new waitress," said Gram, holding Shea's hand in the air. "I've hired her to work a couple days a week after school."

Shea hugged me and took off to help Meg at the display case.

Gram reached for a tray and told me to follow her out the door to the deck. She carried a tray of cinnamon-sugar pretzel bites. In her other hand, she balanced two clear to-go cups of matcha lemonade.

We sat at the far end of the deck. The sun was bright and warmed my skin. I could hear the ocean waves crashing in the distance. I saw a group of children on the beach flying a kite.

She sat the tray down and took both of my hands in hers. "How is Mouse?"

"He's fighting," I said, holding back tears. "Thank you for breakfast. I didn't know whether he could have the pup cup, but I worried that could've been my last night with him. He's still hanging on, though."

"Good, good," said Gram. "And you? How's your head?"

"Surprisingly, I feel better. Tired, but better." I placed a hand on my chest and felt the tension in my body release.

We both sat in exhausted silence for a few seconds.

She looked at me as though assessing to make sure I was telling the truth about my head, like a new mom counting her newborn's fingers and toes.

I took a drink of the matcha lemonade and slid down further into the cafe chair.

"I think I'm going to keep out of the investigation. I'm over it," I said. "I'm going to focus on the bakery, teaching, and the writing club. I have to make some extra money to pay for Mouse's surgery. I can keep working at the radio station two days a week and on Saturdays."

"How much do you need?"

"It's twenty-two hundred dollars, but that doesn't include his physical therapy. He's also going to have follow-up visits at the clinic." The full weight of Mouse's injuries and how it all hinged on me and my ability to pay for surgery hit me all at once. "If we don't do surgery, he'll have to be put down."

I had done well to hold back tears until that moment. As I stuffed a pretzel bite in my mouth, I began blubbering. "I have made a mess of my return. Mom needed me. I should have been here when it happened. I never got to tell her how much she meant to be me. Why did I have to live in Atlanta and pretend to be a writer and impress fake people who I didn't like anyway?"

"Everyone has to sow their wild oats," said Gram, taking my hand.

Somehow, I wound up telling her about reading the spells in Mom's book and the dream I had of her walking in the forest.

I cried even more. I didn't know who I was anymore. "I've made such a mess of my return to Seabrook," I said.

Suddenly, from out of nowhere, Lean Cuisine leaped up into my lap.

"You're one of us," said Gram.

We passed an hour sitting in companionable silence.

Lean Cuisine moved to the table in front of us, lay down, and rolled over to expose her belly. Gram tickled her, and Lean Cuisine used her tiny paws to strike back. I rubbed her orange fur and listened to her purr.

Later, we walked hand in hand back inside the bustling bakery. I remembered that I had a lunch date with Carlisle. I still wanted to know what she knew about Henry Cherry's failing businesses and his proposed development. I suspected that he was the one who broke into the bakery and then hit Mouse, but to prove it, I needed more information.

I looked at the time on my phone. I had just enough time to stop at the turtle hospital and check on Mouse first.

I decided to ride my bicycle, figuring that I could use some fresh air, and it would give me a little more time to think about Henry Cherry, Moriah, and now, Cal.

When I got to the hospital, Mouse was sleeping peacefully. I decided not to disturb him. I stayed at his door and watched over him for a few minutes, then walked down the hall to speak with one of the vet techs.

I left my phone number with the tech and asked that they call me if there were any changes with Mouse overnight. "Oh, is Cal in right now?" I asked.

The tech, a pretty red-haired girl who looked no more than twenty with freckles and blue eyes, frowned and said Cal had been coming and going a lot during his shifts at the hospital. "I don't know where he goes or what he's up to, but he doesn't seem to make his work here a priority."

I looked down at my phone again. It was time to meet Carlisle, but since she had never texted, I didn't know where she planned to meet me.

She was not answering my phone calls and was ignoring my texts. I was worried.

I called Fin. "I'm supposed to meet Carlisle for lunch. She's going to tell me why Henry Cherry needed his wife's money."

"I don't think she's going to be able to meet you for lunch," he said, adopting a soft tone.

"What do you mean?" A sharp pain rose in my chest.

"We found Carlisle face down in a two-pound bag of cinnamon bought from the farmer's market this morning."

"Cinnamon?" My stomach tightened.

"It caused asphyxiation. The coroner estimates she died about an hour ago. Someone held her mouth and nose in it until she died." Fin paused and added that though it was normal for Carlisle to work at the farmer's market in the morning, they had expected her at the law office by ten o'clock. When she failed to show up for a client meeting, her secretary called the police to do a welfare check at her house.

"Casey June," said Fin, sounding even more grave. "There are two booths at the farmer's market that sell spices. This came from Cal's. It's got his name on it."

****

I rode my bicycle back to the bakery. *How could Fin be sure about Cal?* My mind was racing, searching for answers. *Anyone could have bought Cal's spices.* It was late in the afternoon, and I could see that someone had turned the sign on the front door to "closed."

Inside, I walked up the spiral staircase and into the apartment. I found Lean Cuisine mewing for food, so I reached into the freezer and selected one of the frozen dinners: teriyaki steak. In a few minutes, I brought it piping hot out of the microwave. I let it cool, then delivered it to a very impatient orange kitty.

"My lady," I said.

Lean Cuisine was not impressed.

As she began tearing into her dinner, I noticed that the boxes next to the door where Gram had set some of her things to move back into the lightkeeper's house were gone. In the bathroom, she had tidied up and packed her various creams and candles.

It had been a long day. I was still processing. I know Gram had talked about moving back into the lightkeeper's house. But we were on good terms now, so why was she moving so soon?

I looked over to my bed where Mouse usually lay. My heart hurt. What had started as a tingling sensation in my chest had moved to my limbs.

I slid out of my sandals and threw myself face down on the bed.

Chapter 19

I tossed and turned all night, finally giving up at three o'clock in the morning and forcing the covers back. I knew Gram better than anybody, and something told me that she hadn't moved back to our family's old house as planned. I had to know, and since Gram didn't carry her cell phone with her most of the time and bakeries have to open early, I had a short window of time to make the drive from Nutwood Street to the lightkeeper's house.

I doubted that anyone in Seabrook was drinking their morning coffee yet, much less out of bed. So, I pulled my pink terry robe over the T-shirt and shorts I slept in, then slipped into my Birkenstock sandals. Lean Cuisine was nowhere to be seen.

Downstairs, after making a cup of coffee in a travel mug, I climbed into Bread Loaf and puttered down the empty street. The dark night was just giving way to a deep shade of purple.

Soon, I was coasting onto the road my family used to get to our home. I got out and looked at the gate. I used my cell phone flashlight to look around. Lean Cuisine came sauntering by and mewed as she walked to a nearby shed. This was not unusual, as she seemed to roam freely throughout the island.

I couldn't see the house from the gate, and the gate kept me from driving any further, so I climbed over and walked the rest of the way. Though I was a little spooked at first walking in the dark, I began to relax, gazing at the starry sky. I could smell the ocean on the breeze. These early spring mornings made me think of school being out soon and reading a book on a porch swing.

Soon, our family's weathered home came into view. She looked like an old battleship that had survived storms and fought her share of wars. It was a Victorian home with a turret and a wrap-around porch. Paint peeled off the siding. A neglected porch post bent to meet an overgrown juniper. Though the front door was closed, a screen door slapped in the wind, putting me on edge.

Gram was definitely not there. I turned around and felt as though someone was watching me. I ran with my sandals in my hands the whole way back to the van. To make things more terrifying, when I got to the gate, I was straddling it with my pink robe hiked up around my waist when I noticed fresh blood on the top of the metal gate. *Has someone been here in the time that it took me to walk to the house? Has something happened to Gram?*

I half jumped, half fell from the gate and into the sand and then crazy danced my way into the van. I was sure someone was watching and hoped that they thought I had lost my mind and would stay as far away from me as possible.

****

I sputtered back into the bakery driveway just as the horizon was starting to get light.

I was worried about Gram. I also continued to worry about Mouse. But the White Squirrel Pretzel had so much success the day before that I hated to risk losing customers again. So, despite wanting to crawl back into bed and stay there all day, I decided that the only way I

155

knew to pick myself up by the bootstraps was to indulge once again in some of Mom's clothes. I showered in a hurry, then moved clothes hangers back and forth in the closet until I found what I was looking for: her lilac, hemp strappy jumpsuit. It was vintage, soft, and lightweight. I loved the way it felt on my skin.

Paired again with the Birkenstocks, I felt like I was being myself, maybe the person I was meant to be all along, and smiled. I decided on the fly to take a selfie in front of the full-length mirror. If getting dressed in colorful, soft clothes that flattered your body every day was wrong, then I didn't want to be right.

I texted Brie the photo and sent a message:

—Still feeling the weight of everything. Decided to wear this cutie. You know, it helps. It's like Mom is here with me.—

Downstairs in the bakery, I preheated four ovens and headed to the stovetop to start the yeast mixture. I didn't see texts from the night vet tech, so I decided to call. I found out that Mouse was still stable and had had a good night.

The next hour I spent bringing in fifty-pound bags of flour, making dough, kneading dough, and finally, making pretzels.

By six o'clock, Meg Kidwell walked in the door. It was a surprise to me. I thought her help was a one-time deal arranged by Gram.

I was glad to be wrong.

Meg put her arm around me and asked where she could start. "I plan on making this a permanent part of my week. I'll let Blake pour the wine. Besides, I'd rather be over here with the food."

Customers started coming in for breakfast, and it

was the same as the day before. Townspeople who had lived in Seabrook for decades were catching up with friends over coffee and breakfast pretzel sandwiches. Tourists were enjoying tables on the deck overlooking the ocean.

Meg and I took turns at the cash register. I had just helped a man with a large to-go order when Henry Cherry, Moriah's husband, walked in. He seemed agitated. I watched him pour coffee at the self-serve bar and then spill creamer on his shoes. He walked to the front with his coffee cup and the carafe containing the creamer to complain to me. "This carafe slipped from my hands. Someone needs to be wiping down items and better attending to the needs of customers."

I noticed he had some sort of injury on his forearm. It was wrapped in gauze.

I took the carafe from him and apologized. "Your coffee is on the house, Mr. Cherry."

"Oh, I remember you," he said. "You're the one who came to my office on Jekyll Island to ask questions about Moriah. Listen, I've heard that you've been bothering a lot of people around town. You need to mind your own business."

With that, he set his untouched cup of coffee on the counter and left.

****

By ten o'clock, the breakfast rush was over, and we had three customers still lingering. I made sure that Meg would be okay by herself, then left to go check on Mouse at the turtle hospital.

When I got there, Mouse was much the same as the day before. Some of the swelling had gone down in his eyes. He could peek out a little and see me better. But he was still pitiful.

I sat with him for about two hours. He moaned and grunted as I stroked his nose and very gently rubbed between his ears.

The vet tech came by to say that Mouse had surprised a lot of people, the way he fought. They would keep giving him pain medication and changing his bandages. The veterinarian would operate after I made a deposit for half of the cost of the surgery.

That was hard to swallow. I was hoping they could do the surgery, and I could somehow make payments. I didn't know how I was going to pay for it.

Business had improved at the bakery, but we were still going to be operating in the red for a while. Also, I didn't know how much more money I would need to pay Kit for taking on the lawsuit.

That left me doing mental math as I pulled out of the turtle hospital parking lot. The college paid me once a month for my work as an adjunct professor, so I could expect a check for roughly $700 next week. That left my side hustle at the radio station. I had already put in some hours. If I asked to pick up a few more shifts this week, maybe that would get me at least $400, then I would have enough to pay for half of Mouse's surgery.

With that weighing on my mind, I decided to go see Lindy at the station.

When I walked in, she was wearing an army green sweater with an obnoxiously large jaguar pendant dangling from a gold necklace around her neck. Though the sign outside said no smoking, she was putting out a Virginia Slim.

She came around her desk to hug me. "Casey June, what a surprise. I heard about Mouse. How are you holding up?"

"I just left the turtle hospital where he's staying. He's hanging in there," I said. "They will have to do surgery. That's why I'm here. Can I pick up a few extra shifts this week?

"Of course."

"Also, listen, before Carlisle died, she insisted that Henry Cherry had something to do with Moriah's death. I found out Moriah was considering opening up a storefront for her Beet Boxes. Henry had plans drawn up for the development."

Lindy leaned in to listen. "Do you think that's who was supposed to meet her at the gate the day she died?"

"I don't know." I shrugged.

"I have access to Henry's calendar," she said. "Pull up a chair."

Lindy could barely type with her long, candy-apple red nails, but after a few backspaces, she got into not only Henry's calendar but also his email. First, there was a note on his calendar to stop at Moriah's office the day she died. Just below, there was a reminder to go to the development site, which would have been along the road to my family's home. That would put him at the gate at the time of the murder.

Lindy also pulled up an email Henry sent the same day to Moriah. He threatened not to sign the final divorce papers unless she agreed to use her family's money to become an investor in the strip mall that would house Beet Box.

"Looks like he wanted in on the Beet Boxes, too," said Lindy in a snarky tone.

Chapter 20

Later in the afternoon, I helped Meg as we closed the bakery for the day. We took inventory of the pretzels in the display case and made a list of what flours and other supplies we needed to order later in the week. She helped me wipe down tables and clean the kitchen.

I loved being with Meg for a lot of reasons. Her warmth. The way she was easy to forgive people. But mostly, she was the same age as my mother, and she was Brie's mother. Though we had always been close, these last few years since Brie's disappearance and then Mom's accident had brought us closer than ever.

She turned to me as she untied her White Squirrel apron. "You've done so much for me and Blake these last few days. I had stopped keeping Brie alive. I had given up on her. You've given me my hope back."

I smiled, then decided to confess to her that I had been writing to Brie all these years. "I still text her."

Tears welled up in Meg's eyes. "Oh, honey," she said, bringing me in for a hug.

She released me, and I pulled out my phone. "Every day. I tell her what's going on, how we miss her, what's changed, what's stayed the same."

"Do you think she's still alive?" She let that last word hang in the air. "After all this time."

"I don't know. I keep thinking back to that night that she disappeared. She was happy, and we were looking forward to so many things."

"She was supposed to come home that next week," said Meg, pulling out a tissue from her pocket and dabbing at her eyes. "I had bought her some new summer clothes. I knew she wasn't in high school and could pick out her own clothes, but I wanted to have something special for her when she came home."

She cried a little more, then added, "I kept those clothes out on her bed that first year. Then, Blake said we had to move on, and we put them away together. After the Cocktails and Trails event, and so many people offering to help with a new search, I got those clothes back out."

We hugged each other once more. Then, Meg remembered to ask about Gram.

"Any word?" she said.

I let out a heavy sigh. "No, but I know Gram. She'll be back. I just hope she knows what she is doing. And that she won't be in trouble when she gets back."

****

I had promised Fin that I would come by the police station to answer follow-up questions. That would be a good distraction from the mess my life had become.

I was going to ride my bicycle to the station, but out of curiosity, I wanted to look in first on Nissy's book hunt. I had been following her social media page all week; there were still no posts showing that townspeople had found the loot.

I left my bike chained to the railing on the bakery porch and carried my bag with me. I walked quietly along the path where Nissy had hidden the books and gift cards. First, I passed by the birdhouse and saw that it was on the ground once again, splintered wood everywhere and book pages blowing in the wind. The gift card was missing.

I continued as quietly as I could along the path, hoping the thief might still be in the area. As I rounded a curve in the path, I could make out a hooded figure pulling pages from a book. The hood covered most of the person's hair, but some frosted pieces had blown out in the wind. I was close enough now to see perfectly manicured hands and hear the smack of gum.

I recoiled, my ribs tightening. It was a grown woman. One of our own. I was beginning to understand Little League parents' rage when they suspected referees of being biased for the other team. *I smell hometown cooking!*

I walked back to the splintered birdhouse and began taking pictures.

Though I hadn't looked at it since the night Gram gave it to me, I could feel the weight of Mom's spell book in my bag. I reached for it and flipped to the spell to make your enemy love you. Half-heartedly, I read the words. Then, watching some of Nissy's torn book pages blow away, something came over me. I read aloud with much more force. Punctuating the last words. I shouted to the wind, "I compel you to transform anger and resentment into affection for your enemy."

I texted Nissy:

—*Got time to file a police report? I just saw your thief!*—

Nissy:—*Meet at my shop. I am filling our to-go coffees right now.*—

****

I drove Bread Loaf with a clatter down the street. In under a minute, I was pulling into the parking lot and walking up to Lemon Meringue. I waved through the glass door, and Nissy was already on her way out with two coffees.

"My lady," I said, holding the door open for Nissy.

"My lady," she said, handing me a cup of coffee.

Nissy nodded toward her 1975 Chevrolet Blazer parked on the street. The factory hardtop had been removed. "Let's take mine today."

Her Blazer was too obviously similar to the one owned by the police chief in that other beach town, you know, the one from Jaws. *At least our small town wasn't dealing with a shark attack,* I thought. But on Amity Island, everyone knew who the killer was and how to avoid being the next victim. Stay out of the water.

In Seabrook, your next bite of food could be your last.

As she drove, Nissy was digging for lip balm in her large messenger bag she called a purse. She had everything in that bag. Pantyhose, crackers, a deck of cards. I noticed something that looked like spray paint.

"What is that?" I yelled, over the wind blowing in our hair.

"Hornet spray. For protection," said Nissy. "It shoots out twenty feet."

"Have you ever used it?"

"Not yet."

When we got to the police station, we asked for Fin, but the receptionist said he was meeting with some other people. We agreed to meet with another officer. I answered follow-up questions about the night of the attack. Then, I described what I had seen at The Book Hunt locations and showed the pictures of the destroyed books. Nissy also gave a statement.

The officer was taking notes and looked up to ask me if I recognized the thief.

I cut a glance at Nissy. "It's the Queen Bean."

"The queen?"

"Her majesty also goes by Donna Jean Brownmiller."

I held up my phone showing the picture I took of the thief's backside. It showed a frosted strand of hair or two hanging out of a hoodie.

"That's a lead, but it's not enough for me to go charge Ms. Brownmiller with anything," the officer said. "We'll have to catch her in action."

With that, Nissy agreed to restock The Book Hunt locations with new loot. She would remind a few of her friends who power walked along that path to keep an eye out. They would call when they saw the thief strike again.

As we walked out of the interview room, we saw Henry Cherry and the college president, Mills Banks, walking out of Fin's office. They were shaking hands. When Henry caught sight of me though, he quickly stuffed his bandaged forearm in his coat pocket. He scowled as he guided Mills to the exit doors.

"Someone is not happy," said Nissy.

After they left, Fin came over to check on us. "How is Mouse?"

"About as good as can be expected right now. They have him on some strong drugs. We will be doing surgery soon," I said, my voice breaking with that last word.

Fin reached out to touch my shoulder, then shifted his feet and went right back into detective mode.

He wanted to know why we were at the station.

"Everything else all right?"

"We know who has been destroying my book hunt," said Nissy.

"I'll give you a clue," I said. "She doesn't wear the crown so well."

Back in the Blazer, I caught Nissy up on everything. Gram was missing. The cost of Mouse's surgery. Trying to work extra hours at the radio station.

Also, everything was pointing to Henry Cherry. I told her about the papers in Moriah's office, how Moriah had cut Carlisle out of the Beet Box business, and the fact that Henry was planning a strip mall and wanted Moriah to invest in it.

"I haven't even told you the worst thing," I said. "They were planning to open a chain pretzel store in the strip mall!"

"No way!"

"Yes way!"

I was feeling so overwhelmed.

With Gram gone and Mouse at the hospital, I didn't want to go back to the bakery and apartment by myself. "Want to come in with me and try something I've been meaning to put on the menu?"

"Girl, please. I'll eat anything you make."

She parked her Blazer next to Bread Loaf, and as we clambered up the bakery front steps, two white squirrels dashed across the deck and into a tree.

The sun was just dipping below the horizon. The late afternoon air was thick with humidity and smelled like honeysuckle. Overhead, clouds were building, and as I looked out toward the ocean, a salty mist seemed to hang above the water, thinner than fog.

Once inside, I got to work. I placed two soft pretzels

on a sheet pan and warmed them in the oven for a few minutes, then brushed them with melted butter and dipped them in coarse salt. I plated them and topped each with a scoop of vanilla ice cream. Last came a drizzle of caramel, a few cookie dough bites, and chopped candied pecans.

Before I brought them out, I snapped a picture. It was time to put these on the menu. I posted to my online followers: "Like salty? Like sweet? Come try our latest dessert. Introducing the White Squirrel Nest."

Nissy's eyes lit up when I brought them out. I handed her a fork and knife. "You'll need both for this. I promise."

We sat at the front window and watched the bright pink and orange sky change to green, then blue and purple. The color of the water dimmed from blue to black.

I couldn't stop thinking about Henry Cherry and his idea to develop the land next to Donna Jean's family estate. What did it have to do with me? Other than not wanting to share the road.

"If Henry did kill Moriah and Carlisle, do you think he is the one who has been threatening me?"

****

Later that night, I showered again to get ready to teach the mystery literature course at Seabrook Community College. Though my days seemed to be double-booked lately with event planning, working the phones at the radio station, and chasing after wayward beagles, I was looking forward to seeing my students and losing myself in good, old-fashioned literary analysis.

After my shower, I was already wearing a tank top and had pulled on gray skinny jeans and black flats. As I stood in front of the mirror, I spied Mom's multi-colored cardigan hanging on a hook by the door. I slipped that on, decided to let my hair air dry, grabbed my bag, and headed downstairs. In the bakery, I packed a box of leftover soft pretzels for my class, some nacho cheese dipping sauce, plates, forks, and napkins. Then I headed outside.

The night air was cool on my skin, and I saw fireflies at the edge of the forest district trail. Clouds had moved in and covered the moon. I looked around for a beat before deciding to take Bread Loaf instead of my bike.

I loaded my things into the van, turned the key, and Bread Loaf's engine began to rattle and roar. Soon, I sputtered into the college parking lot to see students walking to class.

Inside my classroom, a few students were settling into chairs and desks. Some were already seated. I set out the box of pretzels, plates, forks, and napkins. "Please help yourselves. How is everyone tonight?"

"Tired," said one student.

Another answered with, "Ready for the semester to be over."

I shot back with words of encouragement. "Just a few more weeks. Everyone hang in there."

Then, class began. We were picking back up on our discussion of *Death on the Nile*. Tonight, we were discussing motive and how Agatha Christie used red herrings to throw readers off.

"Looking back," I said. "It is quite obvious now that Jacqueline de Bellefort was planning something bigger. She put everything in motion when she introduced her beau Simon Doyle to her best friend Linnet Ridgeway."

At that, Peter, one of the students who spoke up the

most, raised his hand. "Agatha Christie wanted to get that part in early in the story, then find a way to make us think of it as insignificant. She wanted us to focus on the jilting of Jacqueline, rather than the setting up of Linnet. It looked like a cat fight, but it was the same old story, a woman scorned by a man will have her revenge."

There was another hand raised in the back. It was Roxanne, a student who was writing Agatha Christie fan fiction. "Meanwhile, Simon, as they cruise along the Nile, looks to be guilty of nothing more than breaking someone's heart."

Our discussion lasted nearly an hour, then students worked in groups on a character motive chart.

I wrapped up class by reminding students that authors of detective fiction can make us blind to what is usually right there in front of us. "Someone could have motive and means but look the part of the innocent friend or person who wants to help."

As students started to get up from their chairs and zip up backpacks, I let that last part wash over me. What was I missing about Moriah's side business? What was it her husband needed from her so badly?

What about Carlisle? With her out of business with Moriah, why kill her now?

That left Cal. He was a friend to almost everyone in Seabrook. The least likely to be accused of murder. Was my long friendship and complicated history with Cal clouding my ability to see him as a suspect?

Chapter 21

The next morning, the weather forecaster warned of a fast-moving nor'easter coming up the coast. I was still in bed as I read the weather alert on my phone. I looked down to see one of Mouse's chew toys and sighed.

Across town, people were preparing for the storm. Though not a hurricane, some islanders seemed to take it seriously. The storm could bring strong winds and thunderstorms. Some tourists left town a little early. Homeowners bought generators and extra food in case the power got knocked out.

Families who had been on the island a long time paid little attention. I put myself in that group. I remember several strong storms as a child. A hurricane skirted our island when I was in high school. I had grown up watching Mom and Gram light the oil lamps and wait it out.

I walked outside to look for Hazel. A strong fog had formed over the ocean. The sky was overcast, blocking the sun. The briny air mixed with dust from the wind. It smelled somewhat pungent and made my nostrils flare. I sat in a chair on the deck and waited. In a few seconds, my friend made her appearance on the table beside me.

"Hazel, sometimes I don't know what I would do without you," I said, tossing my daily offering to her on the table. She sniffed the piece of pretzel and waited. In what had usually been a house full of animals, I was down to one today. I hadn't seen Lean Cuisine all morning.

"Where do you think Gram went?" I asked Hazel. "I'm worried. I just hope she knows what she's doing."

I looked down at my phone.

Overnight, I received a text from the vet tech. She had sent a picture of Mouse. He was still swollen but slowly looking like himself again.

I texted the daytime tech letting them know that I would be stopping in again today.

Me:—*Do I need to bring anything for Mouse?*—

The tech:—*A stuffed animal or maybe a blanket, anything from home. That might make him feel a little better.*—

I walked up to the apartment and found the quilt top my mom had made and placed it on a bench next to the door. I also prepared a small pup cup. It probably wasn't allowed by the vet techs, but Mouse would appreciate me sneaking it in.

After a shower, I was looking for something to wear and noticed that Mom's faded blue jean overalls were neatly folded on the papasan chair. Gram must have washed them before she left. The stain was gone. I carefully unfolded the soft denim and slipped into the overalls. I paired them with a long-sleeve black T-shirt and my chunky Birkenstock sandals.

Soon, I headed back downstairs to prepare to open the bakery.

With the storm coming and tourists leaving town, I didn't expect as many customers today, so I didn't make any new pretzels. Meg and I had made plenty of bratzels and soft pretzels the day before. There were several large containers with Irish crosses and pretzel bites. I laid out more of each in the front display counter.

Just as I put the coffee on, Meg came walking in.

"Morning," she said, tying a White Squirrel apron around her waist. "You ready for the storm?"

"As ready as I have ever been. There's not a lot of prep this morning. I've already laid everything out. I'm just glad you're here. Want coffee?"

We sat by the window watching the ocean and wind blowing in. It was at least forty minutes before the first customer came in.

When the door opened, we were surprised to see it was Fin. He had on a button-down blue oxford shirt and wore his detective badge on the belt holding up his black jeans.

"We've found something from the night Mouse got hit," he said. "The veterinarian told us this morning something showed up on an X-ray of his stomach. They knew all along it was some sort of small electronic device but didn't think it was something he ingested that night or was relevant to the case."

I nodded, horrified at the thought that it could have injured Mouse further.

"Until this morning, when Mouse, er, passed it," said Fin, raising his eyebrows.

He held up an evidence bag. Inside was a pocket-sized smart phone microphone. It had the Christian rock radio logo on the side.

"We know that Mouse bit your attacker. This must have fallen out in the commotion or was used to fend off Mouse. Then, Mouse swallowed it and likely chased them before being purposely run over."

Before I could say anything, Fin warned me to stay away from Henry Cherry. "We don't have enough evidence to connect him as your attacker. This is a lead. Let me do my job. I'm sharing this information with you because it involves Mouse."

I didn't know what to say next. We had been round and round on this. If I went snooping for more information or asking questions, Fin would be upset. But if I didn't, someone else might die.

"I appreciate you telling me," I said.

I was getting ready to explain to Fin that Lindy and I had been working together and that we had some new information when his phone buzzed. He looked down at a text. "Someone just saw Nissy's thief in action. I've got to go."

I smirked as he left, imagining Donna Jean being handcuffed and an officer having to flatten her frosted hair to get her into the back of a police car.

After the door closed behind him, I turned to Meg. "We haven't had a single customer since opening. The streets are empty. Why don't we just close for the day and let the storm pass?"

"I think that's a great idea," she said. "Do you need anything before tomorrow?"

"No, but I really appreciate you asking."

As Meg made her way out, I texted Lindy and told her I was on the way to the radio station. I had to tell her what the police had just found. I forwarded the message to Sam and asked him to meet us there.

Nissy, as if she could read my mind, burst through the door. I erased the text I was getting ready to send her.

"I closed for the day, too," she said. "I had a feeling that you were closed. You look like you're getting ready to levitate. What is going on?"

"Well, Mouse did his business this morning, and

let's just say he made us a little present."

She raised her eyebrows.

"Come on. I'll explain in Bread Loaf!"

****

We met Sam in the radio station parking lot. He got out of his truck, still wearing his campus police uniform and worn boots. He held open the door to the radio station.

When we entered, Lindy had just started a thirty-minute commercial-free playlist. She had already left the control room and was sitting at the desk out front, opening a box of dog biscuits. Rachel, the smallest of her two schnauzers, sat obediently. Ross scooted his butt across the carpet.

"What a mess this storm is making of things," Lindy said. "I was supposed to get my nails done this afternoon, but they called and canceled on me. Closed for the day."

"That's why we're here. We have closed, too, and we have some new information to share," I said.

Then I spilled everything—the X-ray, Mouse's bowel movement, the tiny microphone.

"Henry carries one of those in his pocket," said Lindy. "He has a weekly podcast, Coastal History. He interviews folks in town throughout the week to get good material, stories people remember from growing up on the island, old landmarks. That kind of thing," said Lindy.

"Fin says it's a lead, but they have to corroborate the evidence," I said.

Sam leaned in. "We need a witness who saw him attack Casey June and Mouse. Or someone who might have seen him with Moriah. Or at Carlisle's house. Without that, they can't make an arrest."

"He'll never confess to it, either," said Nissy. "If we want him arrested, we'll have to expose him."

Lindy twisted side to side in her office chair, then her eyes brightened. "What if we can get him to confess on live radio?"

Chapter 22

The plan was to meet at the radio station at six o'clock that night. That gave me a few hours to look in on Mouse, return home, and prepare mentally. I had changed into what I considered to be my mom's power suit—an army green jean jacket with a peace sign and embroidered daisies, along with black skinny jeans, a T-shirt, and rubber rain boots.

As the time got closer, I laid out the essentials— backpack, water bottle, and rain jacket. I went downstairs to the bakery and filled a pastry box with cinnamon-sugar pretzel bites.

A cup of coffee later, I walked out onto the deck. I was enjoying what appeared at first to be a hazy sunset showing off its colors, but then it dawned on me that it looked more like a warning in the sky. Things began to shift. Within minutes, everything began to get dark. I noticed that an ominous cloud—thick and black—had created a shelf behind me to the south. The sky was a color I had not seen before, and as my throat became dry and the air thin, I was dumbfounded as to what color that would be called.

The only thing I could think of was Faulkner's short story, "Barn Burning." *Didn't one of the characters have eyes the color of storm scud?* Suddenly, the wind picked up, and then a sign for the coastal forest district came blowing past me.

The storm was here.

I heard a rumble of thunder in the distance as I walked down the front steps to wait for Nissy to pick me up. I felt the hair on my forearms rise with the static electricity in the air.

Lindy had given us a window of time to be at the station. She had planned a fake award ceremony to be broadcast on the radio. She would interview Henry first, then present his award for preserving history in our community. She had told Henry that Nissy and I were coming to bring refreshments and that Sam was on the Hometown Heroes Award committee.

I couldn't risk telling Fin. He would only get on to us anyway and tell us to go home. We were too close.

Nissy pulled up just as a bolt of lightning struck in the distance. She had put the hard top on her Blazer because of the storm. The only thing missing was a set of cherry top emergency lights. I felt like I was rushing to save Seabrook from its own great white.

She had her hair in a messy ponytail and was wearing blue jean shorts and had changed out of her Lemon Meringue T-shirt into a button-down pink oxford shirt. She leaned toward the open passenger seat window and waved. "Are you ready for this?"

"About as ready as a cat getting into a bathtub."

Sam got out and held the door for me. I nearly melted each time he did this. I was ready to jump all saddle and tack into a relationship with his Kentucky character and constitution. He was wearing a gray button-down shirt and his tight, faded jeans. He smelled like old leather, vanilla, and nutmeg.

My heart had picked up speed as I piled into the truck. I took a deep breath and tried to look away from

Sam. I watched as Nissy shifted gears, then began to look around.

Her vehicle was loaded down. She had packed everything from refreshments for our fake award reception to flashlights, rope, and a shovel.

"What is all of this stuff? We're trying to get a confession, not bury a dead body," I said.

"In case things go south," she said, sputtering to find the right words. She reached inside a picnic basket and handed me a slice of pie in a see-through container, then a fork and napkin. "We're bakers. We can do anything."

****

We pulled into the parking lot at the radio station just as a drizzle began. We could see that the light was on through the glass door, but no one was at the front desk. I pulled the door open to find Lindy's two dogs curled up in a pet bed on the floor. Rachel, the white schnauzer, cut her eyes in our direction for a moment before closing them back. Ross used his hind leg to scratch his mustache, then rolled over.

The door to the right had an "On Air" sign flashing, casting a pink/red glow over the room. I looked down the hall, which was dark. "Lindy?"

I heard a knock from the "On Air" room and looked up to see Lindy motioning us inside. She was dressed in typical Lindy fashion: crushed black velvet tunic and dangling gold earrings. Her platinum blonde hair had been blown out straight and hung limply along her ears. She wore bright red lipstick.

I opened the door to find her seated at the control table. A song about following your passion was playing. Across from her, Mr. Cherry sat looking down at his phone. He looked up as we walked in and cut me a look.

I used disposable tongs to place each of the cinnamon-sugar pretzel bites onto a tray, then set the tray on a small side table near the control panel. Nissy laid out a turtle pie.

Sam stood nearest to the door. Nissy and I sat down in seats next to the table. She let her purse fall to the floor. I sat my backpack next to my feet.

Soon, we could hear a downpour begin outside. I looked out the window to see palm trees blowing in the wind.

Lindy winked at me and motioned for us to help ourselves to coffee from the pot on the table. Sam poured himself a cup and took a sip.

Then, Lindy hit a button on the control board as the song stopped. "Wow, wonderful stuff, folks. That song reminds me to love myself and to love everyone around me. Folks, speaking of that, in the studio today, we have a special guest, Mr. Henry Cherry. Many of you don't know this, but he owns the station. He has dedicated countless hours to preserving the oral history of the island. That's why today we are honoring him with a Hometown Heroes Award."

"Thank you, Lindy. It is an honor to be here today in the studio," said Henry.

"Why don't you start by telling us about your podcast, *Coastal History*," said Lindy.

"Well, it's really just a collection of conversations about growing up in Seabrook. I don't want that history lost. We have to preserve what makes our small town so special."

Lindy nodded her head, then moved her hand to adjust a button on the control panel. "So tell me, Henry, why are you planning a strip mall then at one of the most historic points along the island?"

"What?" Henry shook his head and stood, looking indignant.

"Come on. We all know that when Moriah wasn't willing to invest in it that you had to get rid of her." Lindy smiled. "She had family money. You were married, but she controlled that money. How ironic that you used the caviar of the South to kill her."

Henry looked over at me angrily as she asked the last question. "I don't know what you're talking about."

Lindy, as casual as ever, reached into her bag for a pink revolver. At this, Nissy and I exchanged nervous looks. *I didn't know this was part of the plan.*

She stood up and aimed the gun at Henry, pressing him again to answer the question. "I think you do."

Henry smiled. "Lindy, if you're looking to air some dirty laundry in this town, you're not one to talk."

At this, Lindy laughed, then turned to point her pink gun at us. She cocked one hip to the side.

I looked over at Nissy, who seemed just as confused as I was.

I raised my hands in unison with Nissy's. I saw Sam crawling out of the room. *I can't believe this.*

Lindy motioned the gun toward the floor. "On the ground. Now, ladies."

We kneeled and were eye-level with the tray of pretzel bites and pie. Overhead, the end of the Barbie gun was bearing down on us.

Chapter 23

The rain had intensified. The wind was howling. Strong gusts shook the building. Through the window, we could see flashes of lightning.

Lindy, still pointing the gun at us, walked over to Henry and kissed his cheek. "I'm doing this for us, Hen. The only things now standing in our way are these two and their campus cop beau, who can't seem to mind their own business."

Henry stuck out his hand, trying to get Lindy to surrender the gun. "Come on, sweetie, give it to me."

But she moved further away. "Shut up, Henry. If you're not man enough to take care of business for our future, then I will."

At this, Nissy looked at me and rolled her eyes. I felt like I had gone to one of my high school friends' houses, and their parents were getting into an argument.

Lindy turned back to us, fussing with a necklace beneath her tunic. "Ladies, don't think that your knight in shining armor is saving you right now. That coffee may have been stout enough to make your britches stand on their own, but it was laced with a half a bottle of dog tranquilizers."

My stomach dropped. I'd had enough. "Why are you doing this? If it's Henry's businesses that are in trouble and his proposed development that is jeopardized, why are you risking it all?"

Then, Lindy made a big show of glorifying her affair with Henry. "I wanted to get rid of Moriah because she refused to invest in the development. The strip mall needed an anchor store like Beet Box to be successful.

"If I killed her, Henry would get her family's money and the life insurance money because he was still married to her," said Lindy, smiling. "Henry and I had been planning that development ever since Donna Jean's mother passed away. We saw that as an opportunity, a great location. Then all I needed to do was marry him."

I was putting everything together. "So, you asked him to kill Moriah, and when he refused, you did it yourself. You knew she was severely allergic to peppers. I guess Carlisle found out?"

"That nosey old bag with punky hair. She was going to tell you everything, and I had to stop her."

Lindy held the gun in one hand and reached for her purse to grab her lipstick with the other. She flicked the top off her lipstick and began applying it. Her sleeve rode up, revealing a dog bite that was still red and swollen.

I held back tears. "It was you who threatened me. You broke into the bakery. That night on the front steps, you attacked me, then purposely hit Mouse."

"Didn't your mother ever tell you that no one likes a know-it-all?"

"No, my mother raised me to take care of this town." Tears welled up in my eyes.

"Your mother and your grandmother wore those hippie clothes," said Lindy, laughing now. "Your family bakery is losing money. That house on the coastline is a heap. The family legend. Total bunk. Don't get me started on that tubby mutt of yours."

She looked down to put her lipstick back in her

purse.

Nissy saw this as an opportunity. Still kneeling, she used her palm to flip the tray of pretzel bites up into the air. Everything went flying in a blur of motion—pretzel bites, loose sugar, the tongs, a few napkins.

This did little more than get sugar on Lindy's face and make her wince and stumble back. But it was just enough of a distraction.

I looked down to see Nissy's bag on the floor, gaping open as usual. I muttered something about a charley horse and rose up with Nissy's hornet spray, laying down hard on the nozzle. A steady stream spilled onto Lindy's ruby lips and caused black mascara to run down her cheek.

Lindy squealed and dropped her pistol. Henry, in the commotion, took off running. I heard a car start outside and wheels spinning as he tore out of the parking lot.

Lindy was having trouble seeing as the bug spray mixed with her make-up, tears, and snot. Nissy grabbed the turtle pie and smeared it into Lindy's face, knocking her to the floor. But Lindy, crawling around on all fours, somehow managed to pick up her pistol. She rose up with pecans and caramel oozing down her chin and ran one hand across her mouth to belt out, "What is it with you bakers? You think that's going to stop me?"

She waved her gun around as she made for the door, and Nissy and I crouched down behind the table. A shot rang out. The bullet missed us by a few feet, hitting a computer monitor beside us.

She ran out of the station's back door and stepped over Sam, who was unconscious on the floor next to the spilled cup of spiked coffee. Rachel and Ross were licking his face.

Nissy and I chased after Lindy, running outside into a torrential downpour. Thunder rolled overhead, creating an almost constant rumble in the background. The wind pushed against us, and the rain was coming at us sideways, stinging our faces.

Lindy navigated the wooden porch planks in her stiletto heels. Flashes of lightning made it possible to see that she was headed for the stairs at the end.

Then, a bolt of lightning struck so close and with so much force that I could feel electricity on my skin. As the night air lit up, I saw a familiar silhouette—the pointy ears, the arched back, and the long, curled tail. Lean Cuisine was crouched near the end of the last step, waiting!

Lindy bumbled her way down the deck steps. Then, as she wobbled onto the last uneven board, Lean Cuisine rose up and took flight, tearing across Lindy's black velvet shirt.

"Ahhhh," Lindy screamed, waving her gun. "Get out of my way, you feral piece of trash."

Lindy kicked at the cat, which took off running, then missed the last two stairs and fell hard into what had become a small lake in the backyard. Her gun launched into the air during her fall and landed somewhere in the stormwater.

The rain came down in sheets at this point. The lightning had moved off into the distance. All I could hear was rain pelting the porch.

"Mom!" I screamed and searched the darkness all around us.

Nissy caught up to me and looked at me inquisitively. "Who?"

"It's a long story," I said, shaking my head. "Just

help me find the cat."

Nissy dialed 911, and I waded through the soggy mud and grass behind the radio station. But it was quiet, except for Lindy's moans.

First responders made it in about a minute. Fin followed soon after. The quick response time was due to Sam, who had managed to call the police before collapsing in the lobby.

Emergency medical technicians worked on Sam, who was now responsive. He was going to be okay but would have to go to the hospital.

Nissy and I answered questions inside the radio station and stayed for a few hours.

The police had arrested Lindy, but because she had turned off the "On Air" button before her confession, she could only be charged with what she did tonight: kidnapping and attempted murder.

"Lindy has called a lawyer," said Fin. "She will likely go home from jail tonight."

I hung my head. I felt powerless.

****

The next morning, there was still no sign of Lean Cuisine. The storm had passed.

Floodwater still pooled in some of the streets. Sand had been blown like snowdrifts onto the sides of buildings and covered some of the sidewalks.

I decided I needed to get some air, and something pulled me to take a walk to the lightkeeper's house. Without Gram and Mom, I felt the only piece of them that remained was that house, our family's house, where so many of my childhood memories had been made.

The air after the storm was clean, fresh, and full of oxygen. The tide had gone out, and the waves were gently ebbing and flowing. The sun was coming up. Seagulls were calling out.

I focused on all of this to put my mind at ease.

I walked to the edge of town, then saw the road leading to our home. The gate was still there. My shoulders slumped.

Then, in the distance, I heard something. A soft mew. I didn't see anything, but as I got closer to the gate, the mewing grew louder. Almost like a distress call.

There, next to the gate, I found her. Lean Cuisine had ridden out the storm under the small shed.

Her orange fur was matted. She was soaked through. Her left ear twitched a few times, spraying water on my legs. She didn't look hurt. I reached for her, and she purred. I took off my jacket and tried to dry her as much as she would let me. We stayed together in companionable silence for a few minutes.

Then, she dragged one of her paws across the mud in front of her and tilted her head to one side.

I kneeled down and moved some of the mud to see a tiny bit of purple plastic sticking up. Moriah's phone. I recognized it from that day in the bakery.

I uncovered it and stood looking at the screen.

I knew it was unlikely, but I had to try it. I touched the screen. The phone had just enough battery charge left. I stood there stunned that an attorney like Moriah didn't have a pass code and also dreading what would likely come next. There was a reason she didn't have one. She had worried that night about driving out here. She must have had her phone ready.

And sure enough, when I touched the screen, the last app that she had used was open. She had recorded her conversation with Lindy the night she was killed.

I tapped the recording. I heard Lindy's nasally voice first. "Too bad you couldn't just give Henry the money."

Moriah was pleading with her. "You don't have to do this. Please, put the gun down."

But Lindy wouldn't have it. "I said, pick up that spoon and eat the pepper."

Then, a shot rang out, probably meant to scare Moriah.

A few seconds passed. The last thing on the recording was the sound of someone choking and gurgling.

Chapter 24

Several days had passed since the storm. Shopkeepers were outside in the early morning light, sweeping palm tree branches and debris from porches. Sandpipers intermittently ran on the beach and took flight. The white squirrels in my backyard were once again scurrying up an ancient, mossy oak tree. The sounds of a small, quirky coastal town coming back to life.

Inside the bakery, I used tongs to place jalapeno popper pretzel bites on our "free samples" plate. Next to it, I had added a notice: *Nightshade intolerance? Don't eat!*

A line had formed at the register. Our weekend breakfast crowd had never been bigger. Every table and chair were filled. The bakery was overflowing with conversation and the clink of forks and knives. I watched as Meg Kidwell walked around pouring coffee while her husband, Blake, restocked our bar with napkins and straws. Locals interrupted them every few minutes to ask about the weather, trade gossip, and to ask what they could do now that a renewed effort was underway to find their daughter and my best friend, Brie.

For her part, Shea was now working weekends and after school at the White Squirrel. I loved having her around. In some ways, it was like having the middle-school version of Brie all over again. I watched Nissy come in and hug her. Shea took her to the magnetic poetry wall to show off her latest poem.

Soon, Fin came in and took a seat and waited for Shea to take his order. She brought him a water, and he jumped up to give her a bear hug. "Dad!" she said.

I looked down at my phone to see an update from Cal. He was at the turtle hospital with Mouse.

Cal:—*He's having a good morning so far. Mouse is beginning to boss us, though.*—

Me:—*What?*—

Cal:—*I gave him the pup cup you had brought in, so now he thinks he's supposed to have them all the time. I gave in to Lord Mouse. I now have whipped cream in the pharmacy refrigerator!*—

I laughed and put my phone down. Later, we found out that Cal's side hustles—selling spices at the farmer's market, stealing Moriah's idea for pre-made meals, even working at the Squirrel—had all been to pay down student loan debt. Recently, though, the turtle hospital had an opening for a full-time veterinarian, and Cal had gotten the job.

I walked over to Fin and laid my hand on his. "How's it feel?"

"What?"

"Having your baby wait on you now?"

We both laughed, then turned our heads as we heard the bakery door open. It was Jenna, heading for the front display case. I had already taken one step toward her, when Fin stood up and pulled out the other chair at his table. "I think you need to sit down."

After I took a seat, I raised my eyebrows. "Well?"

"Remember we got a tip about Nissy's thief the day of the storm. With everything going on at the radio station, I never got a chance to tell you," he said. "That frosted hair you swore was Donna's. It was Jenna."

"Little Jenna from Lucky Beach? Why?"

"She said Nissy's pie shop was eating into their business with their new pie-flavored smoothies," he said, sighing. "Jenna agreed to plead guilty to vandalism and petty theft for a fine and community service."

With that last part, I sunk a little into my seat, remembering the spell I had cast that day along the path in front of the birdhouse. I watched as Jenna was now hugging Nissy.

"As for Lindy," he continued. "She had her arraignment hearing yesterday before the judge. In addition to kidnapping and attempted murder, they are charging her with two counts of murder, breaking and entering, and animal cruelty."

"What about Henry Cherry?"

"He was the one who attacked you at the gate. He was trying to scare you and keep you away from your family's home in the hopes that you would give in to Donna and sign a paper stating she was the sole owner of the roadway and that you had no easement."

"But how does Donna's lawsuit have anything do to with his strip mall?"

"He'd promised Donna a location for Queen Bean if she got rid of your family's use of the roadway and later made him the sole owner of the road," Fin said. "He saw you and your family's use of the roadway as a blemish on his development."

"More like a hair in a biscuit. We're hard to get rid of."

We both laughed. Then, I shifted in my seat because I knew what Fin was going to bring up next—Gram.

Apparently, that's why Henry Cherry and Mills Banks, the college president, had been at Fin's office the day before the storm. Gram took money from the college foundation, stating in an email to Mills that the college's fund never benefited students, only country clubs and their golf courses, where most of the college's events were usually held.

By the time the college found out, Gram had funneled the money into a fund for Brie's search.

This morning, a warrant had been issued for her arrest.

"Casey June, if you know where she is, you have to tell me," Fin said.

I only shook my head.

Earlier this year, I hadn't wanted to return to Seabrook because I was worried I would end up just like my mother and grandmother, but I realized that there was nothing in the world I wanted right now than to be just like them. *Gram had stood up for something. For someone.*

****

Later, we closed for the afternoon, and I headed upstairs with Lean Cuisine. I had planned to go see Mouse at the turtle hospital but wanted to put my feet up first. I was exhausted, really.

I shuffled over to my bed until my thighs touched the mattress, then dropped face-first into my comforter.

After a few seconds, I looked up at the nightstand in front of me and noticed a worn, robin egg blue hatbox.

I stared at it for a beat. *Had it been there before?*

Still lying on the bed, I commando-crawled to the edge and reached toward the nightstand. I was trying to slide the top open when the box crashed to the floor.

More than a hundred gold coins spilled out. They looked ancient. Queen Anne's profile was on one side of each coin, the crown on the back.

A folded piece of paper was sticking up from underneath some of the coins. I froze. I slowly slid off the bed, then reached for the paper.

I unfolded the note to find two words scribbled in pencil: *For Mouse.*

****

The coins were thought to be from a pirate ship that ran aground off the Georgia coast in the early 1700s. I sold them for enough money to pay for Mouse's surgery, to pay back money Gram had stolen from the college, pay all of the bakery's overdue bills, and then set up a small account to fight the lawsuit. The rest went into the fund to find Brie.

"So, Gram is in the free and clear?" I asked Fin as he waited to give Shea a ride home from her shift at the bakery.

"As long as everything is in order," he said. "Once everything is back in their account, the college has agreed to drop the charges."

After Fin and Shea left, I called his brother Kit, who had been handling the lawsuit. I needed to know if I owed any money this month for court fees or motions that he had filed on my behalf.

"Not any longer," said Kit. "Donna just left my office. She is dropping the lawsuit. Something about kindness being like peanut butter: you need to spread it. Do you know anything about that?"

"Uh, that's odd," I said, thinking back to the day I found the destroyed birdhouse and got Mom's book out.

I put my phone away cautiously. *How did I? What*

did I?

I looked around at the empty bakery. Lean Cuisine leaped onto the table in front of me. She winked.

When my phone dinged, I jumped.

It was Sam. He had been at the college all day for training. He wanted to know if I was hungry. Did I want to go to Watermelon Creek? There was going to be a food truck, and of course, wine and live music in the garden. When I didn't answer right away, he sent another message.

Sam:—*Like a date.—*

Me:—*I thought you'd never ask.—*

An hour later, I changed into a black cotton tank top and a purple sari skirt I found in a box at the back of Mom's closet. The skirt had been wrapped around an old skeleton key. I decided on a whim to thread a red ribbon through it and make a necklace.

I was heading down the front steps of the bakery to meet Sam when I saw Fin's truck pulling back up. He got out to talk to me. "Shea forgot something."

I gave the bakery keys to Shea so she could run back inside.

"Also, I forgot earlier to give this to you," said Fin, reaching into his pocket. He pulled out the turquoise heart pendant. "I found it near the sidewalk at Watermelon Creek."

I reached for the pendant and felt the cool touch of Fin's hand.

Fin's eyes took me in. "You look beautiful tonight. What's the occasion?"

Before I could answer, Sam walked across the driveway between our homes. "Hello, ready to go?"

Shea came running out, and in the awkwardness of

the moment, all I could manage to say was "Have a good evening."

Fin walked slowly back to his truck.

I took a deep breath and pursed my lips together so hard my dimples hurt. Then, Sam and I turned to leave. We strolled to Watermelon Creek. There were a few stray clouds in the sky, and each had taken on a pink hue. It was a wonderful evening. A bluegrass band belted out songs about love and loss. The smell of fried food wafted from a funky little turquoise camper-turned-food truck. When I finally made it to the front of the line, I ordered chicken and waffles.

"That comes with spicy pimento cheese. You want it on the side?" asked the woman, taking my order.

"No, just leave that off," I said, cutting my gaze at Sam.

Later in the evening, Sam walked me to the bakery door. We said goodbye. He made an awkward attempt to kiss me on the cheek and moved away. Then, I went for it. *The heck with it. If we're going to kiss, then it's going to be worth talking about.* So, I planted one on him.

He stepped back, shocked, and said something about seeing me tomorrow. I just waved and stood there beaming.

Later, missing Gram like crazy, I made Midnight Seafoam. I wrapped myself in one of Mom's quilts and stepped out onto the deck with my mug. It was a clear night. I could hear the ocean and looked out to see where it met the starry sky. I tried composing a few different text messages to Fin, but every one of them sounded trite or like I was feeling sorry for him.

I decided to text Brie instead.

I told her about the kiss.

Me:—*I don't know what it is. Sam draws me in. He's all cinnamon and hot peppers.*—

I waited a beat. Then, I continued:

—*Fin is as cool as watermelon mint tea. He soothes me.*—

I started to put my phone down and saw something from the corner of my eye. Three dots had appeared under the message that I had just sent to Brie.

Someone was typing.

Brie:—*Sounds like a love triangle to me.*—

A word about the author...

Sherry Youngquist is a Southern writer obsessed with family secrets and the barrier islands along the Georgia coast. She is a member of Derby Rotten Scoundrels, the Louisville chapter of Sisters in Crime, and a member of The Porch, a literary tradition in Nashville where she participates in critique groups and workshops. Her stories explore folk rituals, body dysmorphia, and women determined to love their jiggly thighs. She holds an M.A. in English.

Thank you for purchasing
this publication of The Wild Rose Press, Inc.

For questions or more information
contact us at
info@thewildrosepress.com.

The Wild Rose Press, Inc.
www.thewildrosepress.com